JACK THE CASTAWAY

By Lisa Doan

illustrations by
Ivica Stevanovic

MINNEAPOLIS

Darby Creek
A division of Lerner Publishing Group, Inc.
241 First Avenue North
Minneapolis, MN 55401 USA

For reading levels and more information, look up this title at
www.lernerbooks.com.

Cover and interior images © iStockphoto.com/subjug (mail envelope);
© Christian Mueringer/Dreamstime.com (vintage postage stamp);
© iStockphoto.com/blondiegirl (postage meter); © ilolab/Shutterstock.com
(wood background); © Picsfive/Shutterstock.com (note paper); © CWB/
Shutterstock.com (passport stamps); © Tsyhun/Shutterstock.com (canvas
passport background).

Main body text set in Janson Text LT Std 12/17.5.
Typeface provided by Linotype AG.

Library of Congress Cataloging-in-Publication Data

Doan, Lisa.
        Jack the castaway / by Lisa Doan.
            p.   cm — (The Berenson Schemes, #01)
        Summary: Upon the death of his Aunt Julia, eleven-year-old Jack is
    whisked by his scheming and dreaming parents from Pennsylvania to a
    small Caribbean island and soon finds himself alone on a deserted island.
            ISBN 978–1–4677–1076–3 (trade hard cover : alk. paper)
            ISBN 978–1–4677–2421–0 (eBook)
            [1. Adventure and adventurers—Fiction. 2. Castaways—Fiction.
    3. Islands—Fiction. 4. Parents—Fiction. 5. Eccentrics and eccentricities—
    Fiction. 6. Caribbean Area—Fiction. 7. Humorous stories.] I. Title.
    PZ7.D6485Jac 2014
        [Fic]—dc23   2013011000

Manufactured in the United States of America
2 – SB – 7/15/14

For Ms. Mercele and Ms. Christine Connor, my Roatan landladies, friends, and personal bankers, who spent quite some time observing my failing restaurant and very late rent payments, and were kind enough not to mention it.

CHAPTER 1

In which Jack is unfortunately reunited with his parents

Jack's parents had finally returned from the heart of the Amazon jungle. They stood at the front door, browned and emaciated.

"Jack," his dad said, "we're back. Not any richer, I'm afraid. And as you can see, the intestinal parasites were . . . a problem."

His mom wrapped her bony arms around him. She felt like a skeleton.

"Just a shame about your Aunt Julia," she said. "Doesn't getting run over by a bus seem like something you say *might* happen, not actually *have* happen?"

"Worst luck," his dad said, shaking his head.

Jack detached himself from mom-skeleton. "You missed the funeral. It was a month ago."

"We set off the instant we read the news," his dad said. "The letter was delayed because—"

"Because the post office was surrounded by crocodiles," his mom said.

"They floated in with a flash flood."

"Record rainfall."

"Absolutely horrible."

"That's the Amazon for you."

Jack folded his arms. "You just made that up. Here's what really happened. You got the first letter probably two and a half months ago. You thought, what a shame. Aunt Julia's in a coma, but she'll snap out of it."

Jack's mom stuck her foot out and examined the overgrown toenails poking out of her sandal. His dad looked over Jack's head and said quietly, "Well, she was a tough old girl."

"*Then*," Jack said, "you got the letter from Bill that explained she didn't snap out of it. She died. And that she had left something for you in her will."

"No, no," his dad mumbled.

"Never saw that one," his mom said.

"The crocodiles must have got that letter."

"Then," Jack continued, "you grabbed your backpacks and paddled down the river as fast as you could because you're terrified of having a job; you still haven't won the lottery like you'd planned; and panning for gold in the Amazon, like all your other schemes, was a complete waste of time."

Jack had delivered some version of this lecture to his parents each time they had swung by Pennsylvania in between their get-rich-quick schemes. He kept hoping it would make an impression, but it never did.

"Ah, but the Amazon was not a waste of time," his dad said. "We were able to firmly determine that panning for gold wasn't for us. Though it seemed like such a sure thing when we first thought of it."

"We even saw a school of piranha eat a cow," his mom said in a hopeful voice. "It was our cow, so that part was a shame . . ."

Jack kept them standing in the doorway. He

didn't want to let them in. They'd just bring chaos into the house. Chaos and weird stories about piranhas and crocodiles. It would never occur to them to do anything normal. Like ask him about his grades or find out who his friends were. Aunt Julia had examined his report cards with a sharp eye. She had known all of his friends. But then, Aunt Julia had been a lot older than Jack's mom. His aunt had always called his mom "the shocking surprise."

Now Aunt Julia was gone. Jack knew Uncle Bill wouldn't keep him. Bill was a nice guy, but he wasn't a blood relation. Over the past month, Jack had mourned his aunt and dreaded the arrival of his parents. He might actually have to live with them if another relative couldn't be dug up somewhere else.

"No worries, Jack," his mom said. "We have arrived prepared. We'll put on a proper memorial for Julia. We've brought a ritual mask thingy back from Brazil. It's scary looking, but the man who sold it to us said it's wonderfully spiritual. And your dad has whipped up a rousing eulogy."

"Have I?" his dad asked.

Bill's booming voice filled the front hall. "Thought I heard a car in the driveway. I wondered if you two were ever coming back."

• • •

Jack spent the afternoon in his room, reading a book about poisonous frogs. It turned out that *D. fantasticus* hopped around northern Peru and was prone to panic. Those poor Peruvians—an anxious frog with poison on its skin was a recipe for disaster.

Jack held the book up with one hand and fingered the Saint Anthony medal stuffed in his pocket. Aunt Julia had given it to him and told him that Saint Anthony could find anything. Jack prayed the saint would find him some long-lost relatives like Aunt Julia, people who had nine-to-five jobs and did no traveling whatsoever.

His parents were downstairs speaking with Bill. Jack couldn't hear the whole conversation, just the loud parts.

"Brilliant!" his dad shouted.

"What about his education?" Bill yelled. And then, "That can't be what Julia had in mind!"

Shortly thereafter, his mom burst into the room.

"Jack, incredible news," she said, collapsing on the bed. "We're off to the Caribbean to run snorkel trips. How's that for an idea?"

Jack stared at his book. *D. fantasticus* swam in front of his eyes. "Who's *we*?" he whispered.

Chapter 2

In which Jack is forced to live with his parents, as other relatives could not be dug up

Jack had vowed he would never travel with his parents. He had a severe case of "will to live" that prevented him from risking his life in foreign lands. There was no end to the diseases, ferry sinkings, volcanic eruptions, train derailments, earthquakes, landslides, blizzards, plane crashes, animal attacks, and military coups that could kill a person.

Jack was surprised each time his parents made it back to Pennsylvania. It was a miracle they were still alive. They were more like cats than people. But Jack knew it was only a matter of time before they arrived at life number nine. Sooner or later, they would get ambushed by a lion or swept away in a tsunami. Then that would be that.

So far, his mom and dad had

- panned for gold in the Amazon (which had not produced any gold but had produced intestinal parasites)
- bought a van in Nairobi and took unsuspecting tourists on safari (which might have worked out, had his parents brought them all back again)
- attempted to export precious stones from India (which the US Embassy had called "foolish" and the Indian police had called "smuggling")
- leased an olive grove in Greece and started the Berenson Olive Oil Company (which had fallen apart when his parents couldn't solve the whole "how do you get the oil out of the olive and into the bottle" problem)
- taught English in Japan (which had led to being chased out of Tokyo by

Japanese parents who thought haiku full of swear words were neither educational nor amusing)

- And opened a fish-and-chip shop in Budapest (which had been shut down by the Hungarian health authorities for reasons apparently too grim to even talk about).

More than once, an American ambassador had mentioned to a British ambassador that granting Richard and Claire Berenson US citizenship had been a computer error. The country that had spawned them should take them back. The British liked to cite their "no returns policy."

● ● ●

Jack rested his forehead on the cold plastic of the plane window and stared at the whitecaps dotting the blue Caribbean Sea. How had this happened to him?

His mom and dad clinked their Salva Vida beer bottles.

"Here's to living in paradise," his dad said.

"Cheers," his mom said. She patted Jack's arm. "We have heaps of plans. Shall we tell him, Richard?"

Dread crept up the back of Jack's neck like a thousand baby spiders. Plans. Heaps of them. His parents' plans had the same effect on Jack as telling him, "By the way, did you know the bubonic plague is in town? You should have those swellings on your neck checked out." He had always figured that when his parents ran out of spare lives, their tombstones would read, *They had plans.*

"Tell him everything, Claire," his dad said.

"Right," his mom said. "First up, we're going to bond."

"Who is?" Jack asked.

"Us," his mom said. "You and me, you and dad. It's been ages since we saw you. You must have tons to tell us."

"Oh."

Jack wasn't sure what to say to that. He had made a serious and years-long effort not to know his parents too well. That way, when they died, it wouldn't be any worse than hearing that the neighbor's gerbil had got loose and disappeared into a heating duct. Hard to ignore the smell for a few days but the tragedy would quickly pass. When Jack was asked at school about their untimely end, he could coolly say, "By all accounts, they never saw the elephant stampede coming."

"Second, we're going to make piles of money so we can buy you a pony," his mom said.

A pony?

"And once we get our business going," she said, "we'll sort out this homeschooling thingy."

Great. In a week, Jack's best friend, Zack, would start the sixth grade. Jack would start a thingy. Zack would be on the soccer team again. And Jack wouldn't. Zack might even get to play this year. And Jack wouldn't. Although Jack had to admit, he probably wouldn't have played even if he'd been there.

And what about Diana? Beautiful, blonde Diana, with the light brown freckles across her nose? Even on the day she'd sat next to Jack on the bus, he hadn't had the nerve to talk to her. He had been waiting for the sudden growth spurt Aunt Julia had sworn would happen. Would Zack hang out with Diana now that Jack was out of the way? Jack was well aware that love was a battlefield. He had seen what had happened when Aaron Schusterman had moved to New Jersey. Two weeks later, Linda Carmichael was like, "Aaron who?"

He came back to the present as his mom said, "As soon as we've got a boat."

● ● ●

The plane circled over the long, narrow island. It landed with a thud on a thin runway parallel to the sea. When his parents first mentioned the Caribbean, Jack had been delusional enough to think they meant somewhere like the Caymans. A place that had movie theaters and malls. But they hadn't meant that. They had meant "the undiscovered Caribbean."

Jack had read about the place on the internet. Both English and Spanish were spoken. The island was inhabited by the descendants of pirates, native islanders, scuba divers, the occasional fugitive, and people who "backpacked."

Jack didn't know anybody that backpacked. Except his parents. But they were British, so it didn't really count. For the millionth time, Jack wished his parents had been born American, like he had been, and that they would take him somewhere normal, like the Grand Canyon. Of course, he reminded himself, if they went to the Grand Canyon, his mom and dad would probably bungee jump into it.

His parents got through immigration after swearing they had just come for a two-week holiday. Jack mentally checked off crime number one.

They dragged their bags to customs, and with the aid of a forty-dollar tip, his dad explained why three people would need twenty-five sets of snorkel gear. Crime number two and they weren't even out of the airport.

The small, unair-conditioned taxi wound up and down hills and screeched around the tight turns of the island's narrow roads. They sped past the ramshackle town of Manda, where houses stacked on steep slopes appeared to hang by their wooden fingernails. Trees as big as oaks, covered with shiny green leaves, stretched thick branches overhead.

They were headed to a village called Lee Beach.

The sky darkened as the sun dipped below the trees. The thick, humid air smelled of wood smoke.

The paved road turned to sand at a T-shaped crossing. The taxi faced the beach, idling next to a stone building with a sign that said Blue Bay Convenience Store. The driver said, "Which way? Where you going?"

"We don't know, actually," Jack's mom said. "We need a place to stay."

Jack pressed his lips together. They hadn't even made reservations. So this was what his parents did when they went to a foreign country. Just arrived.

The driver asked what kind of hotel they were looking for. Jack's mom told him that their top priorities were cheap price and an indoor loo. Then she explained that a loo was a toilet.

JACK THE CASTAWAY

The driver muttered, "Gringos," and swung the car to the left.

The taxi bounced down the rutted road. A whitewashed church, topped by a brass bell, sat at water's edge. Outdoor restaurants on either side of the lane were painted with pictures of palm trees, fish, and coral reefs. Workers lit tabletop candles, and a few sunburned tourists wandered along the beach.

The sun dropped fast to the horizon. The pale blue sea deepened to a turquoise splashed with patches of dark purple. Jack wondered what the dark patches were. Bull sharks, probably.

The taxi pulled into a dusty courtyard, laid before a white stone building with a red tile roof. A blue-and-green sign filled with flying parrots read The Deep Water Inn.

The manager of the hotel agreed to take 150 bacsira a night for a room that would fit all three of them. Jack did a quick calculation in his head. That was only fifteen dollars. They hauled their luggage up to the second floor.

Jack was afraid to look at the place. He didn't see how it was possible to even rent a tent

to sleep in for only fifteen dollars. He braced himself and went in.

The rectangular room had whitewashed walls and a dark tile floor. One frail-looking bamboo table leaned near the door. Three beds were pushed up against the walls. Each had a white clump of fabric hanging over it.

Jack peered into the bathroom. The pipes under the sink were surrounded by broken tile, as if someone had hammered through to fix something and then just got bored and

left. A large cockroach stared defiantly from the shower floor. A sign printed in bold letters hung over the toilet: *DO NOT PUT TOILET PAPER IN TOILET!*

* * *

Over the next few hours, Jack learned a lot about living in the undiscovered Caribbean.

The cockroach in the bathroom could fly, and it landed in Jack's hair twice. His dad thought that was funny and named the cockroach Fred.

The sign about no toilet paper in the toilet was no joke. The girl that showed up with the mop muttered something in Spanish that ended with "Gringos!"

The hotel's parrot despised the color orange. Which Jack found out when the parrot attacked his can of insect repellent. Sand flies were the piranhas of the air, and they would attack any man who dropped his guard, which Jack did while fighting off the parrot.

The undiscovered Caribbean had run out of Coke, but there was plenty of banana soda, which tasted like bubble gum.

A man named Jed wanted to sell one of his boats. His T-shirt said "Jed's Dive Shop—We haven't lost anybody yet!" Jack's parents thought that was hilarious, and they bought Jed a lot of beer. They also bought themselves a lot of beer, so Jed wouldn't have to drink alone.

And lastly, the clump of fabric hanging over Jack's bed had to be unraveled and tucked around the mattress so that mosquitoes would not give him malaria. As an added benefit, the net would keep Fred away from him during the night.

Jack drifted to sleep listening to the drips plopping out of the old air conditioner and thinking about Aunt Julia and Pennsylvania.

● ● ●

Jack woke up and blinked. He was trapped in a white cocoon. Was he dead? No, it was the mosquito net. In the moment of waking, Jack had forgotten he wasn't in Aunt Julia's house in Pennsylvania anymore.

He was in the Caribbean. With his parents.

Jack rubbed his eyes and fought his way out of the net. The room was empty. A short stack of bacsiras and a note in his mother's handwriting lay on the table.

Morning, Jack! We're off to see Jed about the boat. Here's 80 bacs. Buy candy and explore!

Explore? Who did they think he was? Christopher Columbus? Where was the supervision? The whole island could be filled with pirates and hardened criminals on the lam. And who tells a kid to have candy for breakfast?

The kid is supposed to ask for candy while the adult says, "Absolutely not. It's Cheerios or nothing."

Jack peeked around the door and checked the shower floor. No sign of Fred. After an icy shower, he turned off the air conditioner, which sounded as though it was about to turn itself off anyway.

The courtyard was quiet, except for a pretty woman mopping the restaurant floor in slow motion and a girl with her head resting on the wooden counter. Jack woke the girl, ordered toast and pineapple juice, and took his breakfast out to the jetty in front of the hotel.

Two skiffs tied to the pilings floated motionless on the still water. Jack sat on the dock and watched slender silver fish dart around the shadows cast by the hull. An orange starfish stretched out on the white sand. He ate his toast and sprinkled the last pieces over the fish.

It occurred to Jack that Zack's parents might agree to adopt him if they found out he had already nearly lost his life at the claws of a deranged parrot.

Jack pulled out his cell phone and speed-dialed Zack.

It wasn't ringing. He pulled it away from his ear and looked at the screen. No service.

At the end of the dock, Jack tried again. No service.

The middle of the road. No service.

Great. He'd have to e-mail instead. Jack crossed the road back to the hotel.

Across the courtyard, a sign read, *Oficina*. There was nobody inside, but a young couple sat on the steps in front of the door. Jack asked them if they knew where to find the internet.

"What'ya reckon, Kelly? Did we see any signs?"

"I reckon we did," Kelly answered. "Either here or in Guatemala."

"Sorry, mate," the man said. "But hey, Kel, who was the bloke we met last night? The one who said he knew where to find everything?"

"Jonas, babe. He's a local guy. Works in the restaurant next door."

"Thanks," Jack said. He figured the couple must be some of those backpackers he had read about. What else could explain that they'd been to Guatemala?

Jack spent the next few hours talking to Jonas Babe. Jonas said he needed a thirty-bacsira tip for finding the internet, tried to get Jack to book a fishing trip, told Jack he could get him a discount on beer, asked Jack if he had any sisters that wanted to get married, and finally said he didn't know anything about the internet.

It was noon by the time Jack headed out to the sandy lane that ran through the village.

Hand-painted signs leapt out at him everywhere. Jack hurried down the rutted road at a fast clip, alternately reading signs and watching his feet so he didn't trip in a hole. Jewelry for Sale! Open Water Certification Starts Today! Island-Style Cooking! T-shirts! Mopeds for Rent!

No signs for the internet.

Jack had just passed the church. The Blue Bay Convenience Store was directly ahead. He stood in the middle of the road, not sure what to do next.

A voice came from nowhere. "You lost, baby?"

CHAPTER 3

In which Jack does exactly what Aunt Julia would have advised against

Jack looked around. All he saw was a wooden house with a sign that read, Apartment for Rent.

Soft laughter came from above. "Child, I'm up here."

The top half of an older woman leaned on the rail of a second-story porch.

"Oh, hello," he said. "Can you tell me where I can find the internet?"

The old woman shook her head. "You better come up."

Jack hesitated. Aunt Julia had warned him about strangers, although she had mentioned

that middle-aged men in vans were the ones to watch out for. She had specifically warned him to run if anybody said they had lost a puppy. She had not said anything about old women on porches.

"I don't bite, child."

He had to e-mail Zack.

Jack climbed the stairs tucked under the house.

The woman sat on a wooden stool. She pointed to another stool and said, "Rest your bones, baby; it's a hot day. I'll get you a flavored ice."

"Oh. No thank you," Jack said. "I'm not supposed to eat anything from strangers. It might be drugged."

The woman considered this, then said, "I worked my whole life in New York City. I believe that is an excellent policy for the Big Apple. But, baby, this is Lee Beach, and I'm Seldie Moore. I know everybody, and everybody knows me."

Jack didn't think that was true. He didn't know her. So that right there was one fact that blew her story full of holes.

She called down to a young man on the road. "Karl, tell this boy who I am."

Karl looked up and smiled. "Mornin' Miss Seldie."

Seldie turned to Jack. "See, baby? Now, he don't call me *just* Seldie, he puts a *miss* on it. Because he's a boy, you see, and that's respectful."

Jack sat there, not sure what he should do. Should he be rude and refuse the flavored ice or respectful and die eating it?

Seldie laughed. "Never mind, child. Maybe next time. What you came for was the internet. Now, I'm still workin' on figuring out the remote to my television. But I do believe they got to have internet in Manda. Now, if I said I knew *for sure*, I'd be a liar, and I don't like liars. But I say I *believe* because if it is anywhere on this island, that is where it is. I'm forever on a journey to that dusty place for one thing or the other. Just when you think you have everything you need, you go noticin' you need more blood pressure pills. So off I go again and don't dare have a glass of water before I set out or I'll have to go before I even get there. So, baby, that's why it never was a yes-or-no answer. It's a definite maybe."

Jack had tried to follow what Ms. Seldie said as closely as he could, but he got all turned around when she talked about her blood pressure and not being able to drink water. All he could gather at the end of it was that the internet was probably in the town of Manda.

Jack had seen Manda when he and his parents left the airport. It had looked as though a landslide could strike at any moment. And anyway, Jack couldn't go there without his parents.

Or could he?

His mom had left a note telling him to explore. If Jack bought a candy bar on the way, he would be following her instructions exactly.

He could hear Aunt Julia's voice in his head. "Go off to another town? By yourself? In a foreign country?"

Aunt Julia was right. It was too dangerous.

His shoulders slumped.

"What's harrassin' you, baby?" Seldie asked.

"I have to get to the internet to e-mail my friend," he said.

"My advice is, ask the bus driver. If there's internet in that town, he'll know where it is. Do not pay him more than seven bacs, no matter what he tells you. That's the goin' rate."

"Well," Jack said, hesitating, "I don't think I should go on my own. I might get lost. Or kidnapped, even."

Seldie let out a hoot of laughter. "You ain't no infant. When I was your age, there was no road here or taxis and buses neither. I'd saddle up my daddy's horse and ride him all the way into Manda. I loved to ride that horse . . ."

Jack wasn't sure what riding horses had to do with him going to Manda. But Seldie was an adult and she lived on the island. If she thought it was okay . . . And anyway, should he really bother to ask his parents? They would probably let him go to Australia by himself if he wanted to.

"I'll do it," he said. "Where's the bus station?"

"Now there's the conwenience of it. Just stand on the road wherever you happen to be and wait for a bus to come along."

Jack thanked Seldie and went down the stairs and to the road. He stood there with a knot in his stomach. The decision to go off by himself seemed totally wrong, but he was going anyway. The only person in the whole world that would know where he went was an old woman he had just met.

"Wave your arm, baby," Seldie cried from the porch. "Flag them down."

A white van barreled down the road. Not a bus. Jack waved his arm anyway.

The van slowed to a stop, and a boy opened the door.

Jack got in and Seldie called, "Take that boy to the internet. Only seven bacs, mind."

. . .

Jack huddled in a seat next to the window. The van wound up and down hills and around curves, taking the same road the taxi had traveled the night before. It occurred to Jack that he was in a van driven by a middle-aged man, exactly what Aunt Julia had told him not to do. At least there were other people in the vehicle. A young man with blond dreadlocks chatted to a tangle-haired woman who looked as though she might have dreadlocks soon.

The woman said, "I'm a bit nervous about learning to scuba dive, but wouldn't it be brilliant if we saw a whale shark?"

"We might, actually," the man said. "My guidebook says this is the right time of year."

Whale sharks? Sharks as big as whales? Everybody was so scared of great white sharks. How had *whale* sharks escaped their notice? How many people were swallowed whole every year?

The bus screeched to a stop. The boy tapped Jack's arm. "That's you," he said.

There it was. Right outside the window. A two-story stone building with a big sign: Internet Café. He had done it.

Jack paid the boy and ran up the steps. The café was a small room, the walls lined with clunky-looking computers. The girl at the counter told Jack he could log on and pay when he was finished.

The dial-up seemed to take forever. Finally, he got on his Gmail account and wrote to Zack.

You have to get me out of here. This is what's happened so far:

- *Landed safely. (Barely, the plane wasn't much bigger than the one hanging from your bedroom ceiling.)*
- *Parents lied to both immigration and customs. (Yes, they have now involved me in two crimes, so I may be wanted by the authorities.)*
- *I had a banana soda. (It tastes like bubble gum.)*
- *There is a cockroach the size of a hamster stalking me in my room. (My dad named him Fred.)*
- *I was nearly killed by a parrot. (They are more dangerous than they look!)*
- *I have just found out that there are sharks as big as whales circling the island. (I know. They make great whites sound like goldfish.)*
- *Also, while D. fantasticus lives in northern Peru, this island's habitat is similar. (I am convinced they are here.)*

The next time you are standing anywhere near Diana, loudly discuss how I am living worse than the Swiss Family Robinson but am surviving. You could also mention I am using a speargun to catch my own fish. I'm not, but for all I know it may come to that. I am officially a dropout—my parents have not made any plans to enroll me in school. I feel illiterate already. They have actually talked about homeschooling! (My mom calls it 'the home-schooling thingy.') If I am homeschooled by them, I will only learn about the cost of a cup of coffee in Budapest and the train schedules in Greece. This will not get me into college. Tell your parents that I am available for adoption, am in grave danger, and would be a loving son. I hope you are not sitting next to Diana on the bus. If you are, cut it out!

Jack surfed around the internet to see if there had been any plane crashes, capsized ferries, earthquakes, or gruesome animal attacks since he'd left Pennsylvania. He read about a woman in California who was stalked by a mountain lion while riding her bike and a toddler in Ohio who got stuck in a pipe in his own backyard. Both survived. The parents of the toddler said he had done that two times already and they were sick of it. Jack logged off and went to the counter.

The girl checked his time. "Seventy bacs."

"Seventy?" Jack asked. That couldn't be right. His parents had only paid 150 for a whole hotel room. "You mean seven?"

The girl looked bored as she pointed to a handwritten sign on the wall: "Five bacsiras a minute."

Why hadn't Jack kept track of how much money he was spending? If he could do it over again, he probably would not have used so many minutes reading about the kid stuck in the pipe. How would he pay her? Jack only had seventy-three bacsiras, and he needed seven to get back to Lee Beach.

He said, "Could I pay you sixty-six now and come back tomorrow with the rest?"

"No," the girl said. "I'll get fired."

"Could I talk to your boss?"

"She ain't here."

"But I don't have that much money."

The girl crossed her arms. "She say gringos are rich. They just pretend to be poor. She say anybody that don't pay the bill can get arrested by the *policía*."

The *policía*. The police. The girl glared at him as if he were a criminal. Did she know his parents?

Jack dug his money out of his pocket and handed it to her. "Here," he said. His parents might not mind being thrown in jail in foreign countries—they were used to it—but he doubted he would survive even one night locked up with bank robbers and criminal masterminds.

The girl slowly counted out the money, gave him three bacsiras back, then said, "Thank you for your business. Come again soon."

● ● ●

Jack stood on the balcony of the internet café, clutching the railing. It was late in the afternoon already.

Would his parents panic when he didn't show up for dinner? Probably not. They might have already forgotten they'd brought him along. Jack could picture a week going by before his mom would say to his dad, "This shirt looks too small for you." His dad would say, "That's not my shirt." Then they'd look at each other, slap their foreheads, and say, "Jake! . . . No, that's not right. Jack!"

A phone. He could call the Deep Water Inn and tell them what happened. They could send someone to pick him up.

Jack went back into the café. "Could I use the telephone?" he asked.

The girl peeled off a long strip of white nail polish and flicked it into the air. It landed on the counter between them.

"It costs ten bacs."

Jack staggered out of the café.

He stood at the side of the road for what seemed like hours. A few cars passed by as he waited. The sun began to sink. Just as it had done the day before, it barreled down the horizon at warp speed.

Jack's mouth felt sticky and dry.

Finally, a white van rounded the corner. It

was a different driver, and a different boy slid the door open.

Jack said, "Um, I need to go to Lee Beach, but I only have three bacsiras. Could I pay you the rest when we get there?"

The boy looked at the driver. The driver threw up his hands and yelled something in Spanish that ended with "Gringos!" The door slammed shut.

Jack guessed that was a "no." He'd just have to put one foot in front of the other and start walking.

The sky turned a shade darker with each step he took. Overhead streetlamps blinked on, bracketing long stretches of gloomy twilight. A dog barked as Jack passed a compact stone house. It sounded like it had been infected with rabies. Jack fingered the Saint Anthony medal in his pocket. He had asked the saint to find stuff before but never the way back to a hotel.

The occasional car or pickup truck sped by. Jack considered hitchhiking but decided he'd made enough bad choices for one day. He had seen a horror movie once with hitchhikers in it.

A number of young lives had met sudden and gruesome ends.

A flapping noise erupted overhead, and the sky filled with rushing black wings. Jack ducked to the ground. A hoard of bats flapped over the trees. Vampire bats, probably.

Three steps later, Jack heard a loud crunch. He lifted up his sneaker and looked down. A flattened tarantula lay twitching on the tarmac.

Rabid dogs. Vampire bats. Spiders as big as the palm of his hand. What else lurked in the darkness? Snakes. Of course there would be snakes. One deadly strike and the venom would course through Jack's body. He didn't even have a pen and paper for a last will and testament. He would have to use his last breaths to crawl to the side of the road and scratch out in the dust, *Thanks, mom & dad.*

Hitchhiking was starting to seem like a good idea.

CHAPTER 4

In which Jack attempts to teach his parents a lesson that they utterly fail to grasp

The sound of a car engine rumbled in the distance. Jack turned. Headlights careened around a bend in the road. They seemed to fly on their own through the darkness. Jack waved his arms.

The vehicle whooshed past him, blowing his hair back. The brakes squealed, and red taillights traveled back toward Jack.

It wasn't a car. It was a pickup truck. The bed was packed with men crouching next to one another. Their grave faces turned to Jack.

"Hello," Jack said. Nobody answered him.

"Oh, sorry. I meant, *Hola, nochas dias.*"

One of the men reached over, grabbed his arm, and hauled him over the side of the truck. There was barely enough room for Jack to squat down.

He fell back as the truck sped off. As he righted himself, his hand touched something hard and cold. The man next to him gripped a long, glinting machete. Jack squinted and looked around. There were eight men on the truck. They all had machetes.

Why had he been worried about dangerous wildlife? He might have had a chance against a snake. Now he was trapped on a speeding vehicle with a gang of killers.

"Please don't murder me," Jack cried. "I'm only eleven!"

Some of the men stared at him. One shook his head.

Jack looked over the rim of the pickup. What were his chances if he threw himself over the side? Not very good. The driver was a madman.

The men had turned away. What were they waiting for? Were they playing some kind of diabolical cat-and-mouse game?

"Get a grip," Jack muttered to himself. Maybe the machetes were for something else. Like chopping wood. Aunt Julia had used an ax to chop wood; it hadn't made her an ax murderer. But then, she hadn't ridden around the neighborhood clutching an ax in the back of a pickup truck either.

The vehicle flew up and down hills and screeched around turns. Jack gripped the side of the truck. He was surprised the men weren't wearing helmets.

The pickup slammed on its brakes. They had arrived at the T-shaped intersection that led to Lee Beach.

The men weren't going to murder him. Not this time, anyway.

Jack jumped out of the truck. "*Muchos grande gracias.*"

The truck sped off down the dirt road.

● ● ●

Bright floodlights lit the Deep Water Inn's courtyard. A few tourists sat in the restaurant, while a middle-aged waitress leaned against the counter and sang along to country music.

There they were. Jack's parents. Did they seem distraught that their only child was missing in a foreign country? Were they on the phone with the US Embassy, demanding immediate action? Were they organizing a search party and handing out flashlights?

No. They were sitting at a table littered with beer bottles and empty peanut shells. His dad pantomimed a story, and his mom giggled.

Jack strode up to their table.

His mom looked up and burst into laughter. "Well, look at you, rascal. You must have had a good time."

"Well done, Son," his dad said.

A good time? Well done? "I'm eleven." Jack said. "We are in a *foreign* country. I have been *missing* for hours. In the dark."

"Missing?" his dad said. "We didn't know you were missing. We just thought you weren't ... here."

"All parents know that if a child has not been seen for seven hours, they are officially missing,"

Jack said. "I am broke. I was nearly arrested. I was practically attacked by a rabid dog. I was surrounded by bats. I had to walk down a road crawling with tarantulas. I was probably seconds away from being bitten by a poisonous snake, though I didn't technically see one. And after all that, I could have been murdered by a gang of madmen with machetes."

"Goodness, Jack," his mom said, "how could we have imagined all that was going on?" His mom glanced at his dad. "And here we were without a care in the world . . ."

Jack clenched his hands. "My blood sugar is low. I need banana sodas. Immediately."

His mom glanced at his dad. Jack's dad fumbled in his wallet and handed over two hundred bacsiras.

Jack grabbed the money and said, "I'm not cut out for the undiscovered Caribbean. Please enroll me in school tomorrow so I have somewhere safe to go during the day."

He spun on his heel, ordered two banana sodas, and stalked up the stairs.

* * *

Back in the room, Jack downed one of the sodas and stood under a cold shower until his skin went numb.

He sat at the rickety table sipping the second banana soda and thinking about what had happened. Yes, it was true that he was the one that decided going to town was a good idea. So that was his fault. But why hadn't his parents looked for him? They should have known that he wasn't the type of person to wander around in the dark in a foreign country, being a rascal and having a good time.

Jack had told himself his parents wouldn't even notice he was missing. But he had not really believed it.

* * *

Jack's dreams were filled with flying bats, swinging machetes, and a police interrogation about why he wouldn't pay his bill.

He woke briefly as his parents talked next to his bed. He kept his eyes shut.

"He seems tightly wound," his mom whispered. "Do you suppose all those things actually happened to him?"

"No way to be sure. But I fear Julia wasn't a good influence," his dad said. "He sounds more like her every day. Talking about his blood sugar of all things."

"Do you suppose he'll grow out of it?" his mom asked.

"Well," his dad said, "let's just hope he grows. I believe he's the shortest person we know."

* * *

The next morning, Jack crept out of the room under cover of his father's snores.

Two hundred yards offshore, gentle waves crested and broke over the reef. Orange buoys bobbed on the other side of the waves. Jack squinted but did not see any whale sharks. The bull sharks sat ominously still. They were scattered across the shallows, biding their time until an unsuspecting bather made the last mistake of a tragically short life.

The sky brightened, and tourists emerged from their cabins and hotel rooms. Jack imagined Seldie got up early too. She probably wondered about his trip to town. She would be shocked when she heard everything that had happened.

Her house was quiet. Jack crept up the stairs and knocked softly on the door.

"Hallooo?" Seldie's voice called.

"Um," he said, "good morning, Miss Seldie. Are you still asleep?"

"No, baby, I don't talk in my sleep. Not that I know of, anyway. Just let me put my teeth in."

Jack settled himself on a stool.

Seldie opened the door. "Child," she said, "how did you make out yesterday?"

Jack had meant to chat about the weather and then casually ease into the nightmare trip to Manda, but the whole story poured out of him. The internet, the money, the rabid dog, the vampire bats, the tarantula, the snake, and the men with machetes.

He had thought Seldie would be more horrified than she looked. When Jack finished, she eyed him thoughtfully. "You poor soul. You got a lot weighin' on your mind."

Jack nodded. "Almost dying gives a person a lot to think about."

"Well, baby," she said, "if nothing else, I imagine it gave you an appetite."

Seldie was right. He was starving. She was a very wise person.

In Seldie's kitchen, Jack helped her warm up leftover rice, beans, and plantains. They sat on the porch and ate in companionable silence.

Jack spent the next few hours on the porch with Seldie. He liked it there. She made him feel calm. She was sort of like Aunt Julia, only not as worried. Seldie told him a lot of relaxing things: she had never heard of a person being arrested over four bacsiras and there wasn't any rabies on the island and the bats ate mosquitoes and tarantulas weren't dangerous and snakes tried to avoid people and the men with machetes were just coming home from work. Jack began to feel like maybe he had not been as close to death as he'd originally thought.

He told Seldie that he wanted to enroll in school as fast as possible, and she thought that was a great idea.

A shriek pierced the quiet afternoon.

"Our son!" his mom cried. "Have you seen

our son? He's gone missing again!"

Jack peeked over the porch railing. His mom collared a tourist and started shouting at him. His dad paced the road, running a hand through his hair.

Jack sighed and put his head down on his forearm.

"Your ma and pa?" Seldie asked.

Jack mumbled into his arm. "Yup."

Seldie patted Jack's shoulder. "You better call to them before they hurt somebody."

"We've only been here for two days!" his mom said. "How can he be missing again?"

"How should I know? You're his mum!" his dad said.

"Hey," Jack called from the porch, "what are you doing?"

His parents looked up to the porch.

"Jack," his mom said, "you're not missing!"

"Of course I'm not missing. Why would I be?"

"Why, you explained the whole thing last night," his dad said. "You're eleven and we're in a foreign country. We woke up this morning, and you weren't there. Then we came back around noon, and you still weren't there. So we thought, uh-oh, here we go again."

"Richard," his mom said, "I think I know where we went off the rails. Yesterday, Jack was gone for seven hours. Today it's only been five."

"Brilliant, luv. That's bound to be it," his dad said.

"But, Jack, where's the cutoff?" his mom asked. "The hour when we decide it looks bad?"

Jack put his head back down on his forearm. How could he answer a question like that? Parents should just know.

"Lord help us," Seldie muttered. She called down to Jack's parents. "The boy's fine."

"Jack, we can stay right here and make sure you don't go missing again," his mom said. "We're absolutely committed to the idea."

Jack picked his head up. "No, don't stand there in the middle of the road. I'm coming."

"Well, all right," his dad said, "but no more stories about being missing when you're just down the road. Your mum and I were off our heads with worry! It's a miracle we were able to concentrate long enough to buy that boat from Jed."

Jack couldn't even guess what Seldie thought about his parents.

Seldie said, "So they bought a boat. From Jed. Those poor souls."

"What do you mean?" Jack asked.

"I'm guessing your parents are the dreamin' type. We get a lot of them down here."

Jack didn't answer. There wasn't much to say. That's what his parents were. The dreamin' type.

He got up and said, "Thanks for breakfast, Ms. Seldie. It's the most fun I've had since I got here."

"Come see me any day, baby. In the meantime, try to relax a little bit."

Down on the road, Jack's mom grabbed his arm and pulled him along the sandy lane. "What a brilliant day we had," she said. She waved to an older island woman. "Evening, Miss Deborah. Jack, we tested the snorkel gear. Wait until you have a go. It's glorious."

"Stupendous!" his dad said.

"And we started the boat," his mom said, "and drove it around in circles. A slight mishap on the first go, but the chap was fine. Just a few scratches."

"He was a good sport, wasn't he, luv?" his dad said.

"You hit somebody?" Jack cried.

They passed Jed's Dive Shop. His dad called out, "All right, Jed?"

Jed waved his beer bottle in their direction. "Another day, nobody lost."

"This island is heaven," his mom said.

• • •

Freshly showered and covered in insect repellent, Jack sat at a table in the restaurant. He watched his parents come out of the room. His dad's thick, dark hair was wet and brushed back off his forehead. His mom was tan and wore a simple white dress. The two of them had gained the weight back they'd lost in the Amazon. If somebody just looked at them and didn't actually talk to them, they would seem completely normal.

Jack was determined to get into a school. A school would be filled with teachers and reliable schedules. It might even have the internet, so he could e-mail Zack every day. It would be a relief to have tests and quizzes to worry about again.

Jack's mom kissed the top of his head. "Hello, luv."

His dad sat down. "Jack. Glad to see you're not missing."

"So, what about school?" Jack asked. "Did you figure it out yet?"

"Why are you so set on school?" his mom said. "We're finally all together. We've found our paradise. We'll figure out the homeschooling thingy as soon as we get the business sorted out."

"This is more than a thingy," Jack said. "My education is at stake. Be realistic. You would both be horrible at homeschooling. I doubt you'd even check my homework."

His dad laughed. "We'd never give you homework."

Jack crossed his arms. "That is exactly the attitude I'm talking about. I need to be in a structured and safe environment during the day. Everything here is dangerous. The land is dangerous, as I found out yesterday. The sea is dangerous. There are bull sharks right in front of the hotel. And did you know there are whale sharks in the area? That's right. I heard two people talk about it on the bus yesterday. Sharks the size of whales."

"Now, Son," his dad said, "you're a bit . . . what is the word?"

"Hysterical?" his mom said.

"That's the one," his dad said, nodding.

"Honestly," his mom said, "even if we were keen on the idea of sending you to school, we couldn't just now. We don't have the money for tuition."

In which Jack explains the value of a checklist

"You don't have the money? How much did you pay for that boat?" Jack asked.

"Oh," his mom said, "it was a really good deal. But the law only lets a person bring a certain amount of cash into a foreign country. The rest has to be transferred by the bank."

"How long could that possibly take?" Jack said. "Just a day or two, right?"

"Actually," his dad said, "Jed reckoned a few weeks."

Jack fell silent.

"Come now, luv," his mom said, "let's not go

on about school anymore. Just give this place a chance. What kid wouldn't love living on a tropical island and skipping school? You can pretend you're Robinson Crusoe."

"Robinson Crusoe was a trained sailor," Jack said. "I've never even been on a boat."

"Ah, we can fix that," his dad said. "Tomorrow, we'll run the boat out for our first snorkel cruise. No paying customers on this go—just a dress rehearsal of sorts."

"And tell him the brilliant news," his mom said.

His dad leaned back in his chair with a satisfied smile. "We've dreamed up a brand-new sport."

Jack felt his face go clammy.

"It'll take the world by storm," his mom said. "Jed told us that just to the north, near the point of the island, a current rips along the coast. The dive shops take their customers there to drift dive."

"It's absolute genius," his dad said. "No kicking required. Just drift along with the current as easy as you please."

"So I looked at your dad and said, 'Are you thinking what I'm thinking?'"

His dad laughed. "And I said, 'You bet I am. Drift snorkeling!'"

Jack fanned himself with a napkin. He felt a little faint.

"So here's the plan," his mom said. "Tomorrow, first thing, we have a big breakfast: bacon, eggs, toast, the works. Then off we go."

"We?" Jack asked. "You don't think *I'm* going with you?"

"Of course we do," his dad said. "Who else would drive the boat?"

"Drive the boat?" Jack asked. "I don't know how to drive a boat!"

"Not yet," his mom said. "But by tomorrow afternoon you'll be a proper boat captain."

"Now, don't thank us," his dad said. "We're happy to do it."

Jack took a deep breath. This wasn't going the way he had planned. How had the conversation turned from getting into a school to driving a boat?

He said, "I don't want to learn how to drive

a boat, by myself, in the ocean, while you're . . . drift snorkeling. The whole idea sounds dangerous."

"Now, Jack," his dad said, "here's what we'll do. I'll drive the boat at first, and then you can have a go."

"It will be good for you to learn about boating," his mom said. "We're living on an island, after all. We won't insist you get in the water. We know you're still a bit wound up about sharks."

"And," his dad added, "a young boy shouldn't spend all his time hanging around an old woman. It's creepy."

"It's not creepy," Jack said. "Seldie is sensible. That's why I hang out with her."

"Sensible, eh?" his dad asked. "*We* didn't tell you to go to Manda by yourself, did we?"

"No," Jack said, "but you would have."

Jack's dad shrugged.

"I'm not going," Jack said. "You haven't done anything to prepare. You haven't thought about safety or anything. You should have checklists, like airplane pilots do."

"Richard," his mom said, "have we ever used a checklist?"

"Absolutely. Remember? The safari business in Nairobi. We had a list of the passengers. We meant to check it before moving from one location to the next."

"You know," his mom said, "I think Jack's on to something. If we had actually used our safari checklist, Mr. and Mrs. Grady wouldn't have spent three days alone with the baboons of Lake Nakuru."

"Quite right," his dad said. "It's settled then. Jack, you're in charge of the list making."

Jack gave up. There was no getting out of it. He had better write up a long and detailed checklist.

* * *

Jack sat at the restaurant table, his checklist laid out in front of him. He had titled it *Boat Owner's Essentials for Staying Alive.*

> *1. Life jackets (minimum of three)*
> *2. Medical kit (including every size of bandage*

and a lot of Neosporin)

3. *Snacks (potato chips and chocolate required)*
4. *Pineapple or banana soda (minimum of two per person)*
5. *Sunscreen (the strongest available)*
6. *Insect repellent (the strongest available)*
7. *Hats*
8. *Sunglasses*
9. *Towels*
10. *Stern lecture from Jack (on topics such as the importance of slow and cautious driving)*

Jack looked from his mom to his dad. "I spent all last night thinking very carefully about everything that could go wrong. You have to agree to follow the list exactly, or it won't work. No shortcuts."

"We'll follow it to the letter," his dad said.

Jack slid the list across the table. "Read through it, and make sure you understand every point."

His parents huddled together over the checklist.

"A stern lecture?" his mom said. "I would

never have thought of that."

"Capital thought, though," his dad answered. "Sort of a 'rally the troops' idea."

"Do we have a medical kit?"

"I'd be surprised if we did," his dad said. "But no worries. We'll pop down to the shop and patch one together."

"Soda! And here we would have zoomed off without it if Jack hadn't thought of it."

Jack interrupted them. "No zooming. We go slow and steady."

"Ah," his dad said. "That advice must be part of item number ten. Stern, indeed. I like it."

His mom gazed at Jack. "Richard, I think we have a very clever young man on our hands."

"No doubt of it," his dad said. "Well done, Jack. First-rate checklist."

* * *

Jack's parents were already on the boat. They each wore a neoprene wet suit and had a mask with an attached snorkel pushed up on their forehead. A green parrot perched on his dad's shoulder.

The boat was smaller than Jack had

imagined. Where was the cabin? It was just a little skiff with an engine bolted on the back.

Jack's dad called, "Ahoy, Captain!"

Jack pointed at the bird. "Where did you get that?"

"Ah! His name is Loco. Nicked him off Jed this morning."

"*Nicked* is British for 'stole,'" Jack sputtered. "Now you're stealing birds?"

"Dad's just winding you up," his mom said. "Jed gave him to us. Said he wasn't very fond of him anyway. I can't think why; he's absolutely lovely."

The parrot glared at Jack and said, "Bad dog."

His dad laughed. "Hah! Funny thing."

Loco preened his feathers.

"I don't have anything on my list about birds," Jack said.

"No worries, Jack," his mom said. "He's no trouble at all."

"Hop on, Son," his dad said. "I'll show you how to start the engine."

"Wait a minute," Jack cried. "We have to go through the checklist!"

"Good grief, Richard, we forgot the checklist already. What would Mr. and Mrs. Grady say?"

"Nothing we'd want to hear, I'm sure. Fire away, Son."

"Okay, listen carefully," Jack said. "No fast driving. High speeds lead to terrible accidents. Think about the consequences *before* you do something, not after. If you're the driver, don't talk to anybody. Concentrate on what you're doing and where you're going. Keep your hands inside the boat so you don't get bitten by a fish.

And the final thing: if we see a whale shark, we turn around and come right back to the dock."

Jack fished the equipment list from his pocket. "I'll check off the stuff we have to have before we go. Watch how it's done so you can try it next time. Life jackets. Check. Bandages and Neosporin. Check. Snacks. Check. Hats, sunglasses, and towels. Check, check, check." Jack lifted the lid of the cooler. "Soda. Check."

"Gosh," his mom said, "what a procedure. It's a lot to remember."

"That's why we have the checklist written down," Jack said. "You can't trust your memory to remind you of every single thing."

"Fine job, Jack," his dad said. "Just the right amount of sternness in the lecture and military precision on the equipment checklist."

Jack passed around the hats and sunglasses. Then he coated his parents with sunscreen while reminding them about the dangers of excessive sun exposure.

"If we keep going like this," his mom said, "we'll never even leave the dock."

Jack's dad yanked on a small black handle. The engine roared to life. "Just that simple," he called over the rumble of the motor.

Jack flung himself down on the bench across from his parents.

He suddenly realized that the boat didn't have a steering wheel. Just a black pole attached to the engine. It didn't even work right. When his dad pulled it one way, the boat went the other way.

"Look here, Son. To head left, pull to the right and vice versa. To speed up, twist the handle. Nothing easier."

The skiff glided over the shallows. Jack peered over the side and into the water. He was surprised to find the bull sharks were actually patches of dark green sea grass.

His dad turned the boat sharp right to face the open sea. Two buoys bobbed fifty feet ahead, marking the channel through the reef. He gunned the engine and said, "Hold on!"

In the channel, the boat dipped front first, then bow to sky, until it rolled down another swell. It was like a sickening amusement park ride. The kind they showed on the news while the anchorman shook his head and whispered, "Terrible tragedy."

"Brilliant," his dad shouted.

"Isn't this great, Jack?" his mom cried.

"Slowly!" Jack answered.

Sharp spikes of coral sat inches below the surface on either side of the boat. Jack had seen a nature show about coral. Falling on it would be like jumping into a barrelful of razor blades.

On the other side of the channel, the waves leveled out. His dad turned the boat left and headed north along the coastline at full throttle. The open sea was choppy. The boat bounced up and down, shaking Jack's teeth.

"Dad," Jack shouted, "slow down! You're a tour operator, not a pirate!"

"Sorry, forgot!" his dad said.

Jack held on and stared at the shore. Every time he glanced away, his stomach flipped.

"Have a go driving, Jack?" his father shouted.

Jack shook his head and kept his eyes locked firmly on land. They passed sandy coves dotted with palm trees. Orange buoys floated outside the reef, marking off scuba diving sites.

His dad slowed the boat to a drift in front of a long white beach. He said, "Jack, you see which way the waves are going? The current runs north. We'll drift snorkel right along the reef, as easy as you please. All you have to do is follow us without running us over."

Loco ran down his dad's arm and plopped onto the bench.

The cove on the inside of the reef was flat and clear. Jack could see the sandy bottom; it didn't even look that deep.

He pointed to it and said, "Why can't you snorkel over there? There's a channel right to the other side of the reef. It looks as calm as a swimming pool. We could put the anchor on the sand and just sit there. That's probably what most people do."

Jack's dad pulled on his fins. His mom was already perched on the gunwale of the boat.

"You've hit the nail on the head, Son," his dad said. "We're not most people. Never forget, we're the Berensons!"

His dad dangled his legs over the side. "Ready, Claire?"

"Ready," she said.

Jack's parents adjusted their masks, popped in their snorkels, and jumped into the water. The current swept them away. They bobbed up and down in the waves like two human buoys. A muffled "whoo-hoo" drifted out of his dad's snorkel.

Jack pushed the tiller attached to the engine. The boat swung the wrong way and barreled toward his parents. He frantically pulled it toward him until the boat was parallel to the shoreline.

Jack's parents flailed and grasped at each other.

"What are they doing?" Jack said.

Loco stared up at him from the bottom of the boat and said, "Bad dog."

His parents had pushed their masks up on their foreheads. His dad spit out his snorkel and yelled, "Bit of a technical problem! Masks have fogged up."

The engine sputtered and coughed. Then it was silent.

Jack pulled the handle to restart the motor. The flywheel turned, but the engine didn't start.

He jumped up, grasped the handle in both hands, and yanked it as hard as he could.

Nothing. Jack paused and picked up the red plastic gas container. It was empty.

He shouted, "You didn't put gas on the boat!"

"Petrol?" his mom yelled back. "Was that on the checklist?"

Jack tasted bile in his throat.

His parents kicked madly for shore. The boat drifted faster along the coastline. The northern point of the island loomed ahead. There was nothing beyond the point but open ocean.

Jack's dad got a hold of a rock sticking out from beneath the waves. He grabbed Jack's mom. They clung to it as the current swept the boat past them.

His dad shouted, "No worries, Jack. We'll borrow another boat and collect you directly."

"Directly," his mom called.

Jack sat stone-still. The boat sailed beyond the northern point. It was like a movie. He was drifting out into the ocean. Could this really have happened? And so fast? One moment, he had been fine. Well, maybe not fine, but just bumbling along through one of his parent's bad plans. The next, he was floating into the middle of the Caribbean Sea.

He squinted at the receding island. Jack's parents had dragged themselves up on the beach.

CHAPTER 6

In which Jack encounters killers of varying shapes and sizes

Over the next few hours, Jack reviewed his situation. He had a box of assorted sized Spider-Man Band-Aids, six tubes of Neosporin, three orange life jackets, a mesh bag full of snorkel gear, a canvas tarp, a book called *Snorkel Now! Caribbean Edition*, six pineapple sodas, six bags of potato chips, six bags of M&M's, three towels, three hats, three pairs of sunglasses, and one green parrot.

The boat rolled up and down four-foot swells. Jack no longer felt sick. Everything that had been in his stomach was now in the ocean.

He stared at the bow of the boat, trying to piece together what had happened. Jack had always known his parents were dangerous. They were like little kids that kept running into the road. Sooner or later, they were bound to get flattened by a truck. But that was the thing— it should have been them on the boat, floating away from civilization. Not Jack. He hadn't invented drift snorkeling or forgot the gas or made an eleven-year-old drive. His parents had.

His mom and dad would have to walk all the way back to Lee Beach to get help. How long would that take? What if the boat sank while he was waiting to be rescued?

He looked down into the water. It was dark. Purple-gray dark. Not like the pale blue around the island, with white sand and patches of sea grass on the bottom. This was just dark. Like there wasn't any bottom.

Jack thought about drifting down, deeper and deeper. That's what would happen if the boat sank. He would get too tired or cold to swim anymore. He would drown. If the sharks didn't get him first.

Loco dug his claws into Jack's arm, ran up to his shoulder, and said, "Bad dog."

Jack jerked his head back from the water. "Yes, Loco, it is very bad. They didn't put gas on the boat. I realize that it wasn't on my checklist, but who would put something like that on a list? I mean, it would be like writing 'Make sure the boat is actually in the water.' Some things are just . . . not on a checklist."

Loco preened his feathers and muttered, "Whatever."

Jack didn't have his watch on, but he didn't need to. The bottom curve of the blinding sun touched the horizon. In moments, it would sink into the waves completely.

Sharks probably attacked under cover of darkness. They might have been circling underneath the boat ever since he had drifted away from land.

Jack put on a life jacket as the sun disappeared into the sea. He lay on the bottom of the boat with the tarp tucked up under his chin. Loco huddled under his arm and softly chanted, "Bad dog, bad dog, bad dog."

A full moon hung heavy and close, as if it might drop out of the sky. The sea had flattened out. It sparkled for miles under the moonlight.

The stars, the moon, the water—everything was too big. Everything but the boat. That was too small.

The skiff heaved and rolled forward. They'd hit something.

Jack sat up. Loco squawked and ran up his shoulder.

"What was that?" Jack whispered. He peered over the side. A large mass, thirty feet long, floated next to the boat. They hadn't hit something. Something had hit them.

The creature's skin glowed in the moonlight, dark gray with pale yellow spots. Its dorsal fin rose three feet out of the water.

Jack sank back down and put Loco under his arm. "It's a shark. A whale shark by the size of it," he whispered. "We have to be quiet. Maybe he'll go away."

The whale shark drifted to the stern of the boat. The boat heaved forward again. The shark was playing with them. When it got tired of

playing around, it would capsize the boat. They would flail around in the water and then . . .

Jack peered over the stern. The shark's mouth opened. It was nearly four feet wide.

"Don't swallow me," Jack whispered.

The shark's head sank into the water and pushed against the stern. The boat clipped across the water. Jack pulled the tarp over his head.

The boat rolled up and over steep swells and then leveled out, drifting more slowly. It felt as though they weren't being pushed anymore.

The hull grated against something solid.

Jack peeked out from under the canvas.

A long beach lined with palm trees stretched away under the moonlight. Jack sat up and turned to face a lagoon. Surf rolled gently over a reef nearby. Jack could just make out a dark area of large swells marking a channel. Beyond the reef, the whale shark broke the surface of the water and then disappeared.

"Loco," Jack said, "it's a miracle. That whale shark pushed us into the channel, but then it was too big to get in after us."

"Whatever," Loco said. The parrot marched over the bow of the boat and flapped down onto the sand.

Jack took the life jacket off and crawled onto the beach. The palm trees cast black shadows on the sand, as if someone had sketched it with charcoal. It was deserted.

He crept under a palm and wedged his back against the trunk. In the morning, he would go get help. And then begin the legal emancipation process.

* * *

Jack blinked awake from a doze. The sky was pink.

Loco strutted on the sand, flapping his wings as if he were drying them out.

A crash thundered to Jack's left. A round, green coconut, the size of a soccer ball, rolled by his sneaker.

He twisted his head and looked up. Clusters of heavy coconuts hung over his head.

Jack jumped up and ran from under the tree. All night he had sat there, coconuts dangling over him, just waiting for a breeze to shake them loose. What would his obituary have said? *While Jack Berenson eluded a notorious killer whale shark, he sadly did not elude a falling coconut. He will be missed.*

He was not prepared to survive in the wild. He was prepared to watch the wild on television while eating Doritos.

Jack's throat burned from thirst. He jogged down to the boat and grabbed a pineapple soda from the cooler. He twisted off the cap and drank half the bottle in one gulp.

Loco waddled up behind him. "Bad dog!"

"Oh," Jack said. "I suppose you want some."

He poured a little into the broken half of a brown coconut shell. Loco poked his beak around the bottom of the shell. The bird looked up at Jack and stared.

"I really can't help it if you don't like it. It's all we have," Jack said. "You stay here while I go get help."

Loco ignored him, swung himself over Jack's belt buckle, scrambled up Jack's arm, and settled on his shoulder.

"I wasn't going to mention it when I thought we would be eaten by a whale shark," Jack said. "It seemed like the wrong time. But I don't really like parrots. I had a bad experience with a certain parrot and a certain orange can of insect repellent."

Loco dug his claws into Jack's shoulder and said, "Whatever."

Jack looked around to get his bearings. The waves ran north, and the sun had risen over the inland treetops, so he must have landed on the west side of the island.

The northern side of the beach rose to a rubbly slope, dotted by gnarled trees. The lower branches of one of the trees overhung a dark opening that looked like a cave.

To the south of Jack, a dark lagoon cut across the beach and disappeared into the trees. The inland slope there was thicker with trees than the northern side, but not as steep.

Maybe if Jack headed up through the trees, he would find a path. A path would mean people.

He turned around to get a soda for the hike. The tide had risen and the boat was afloat, drifting away from shore.

Jack sprinted toward the sea. Loco squawked and flapped onto the sand. Jack waded up to his waist, grabbed the bow, and dragged the boat back onshore. He sat down, breathless. What if he hadn't been looking? All his supplies were on board.

He decided he'd better pull the boat into the lagoon and secure it.

The boat scraped the bottom of the lagoon and threw up clouds of silt. Squat trees surrounded the shallow inlet. Jack tied the bowline to a sturdy branch stretching out over the water.

• • •

Back at the beach, Loco waddled over to Jack and raised a claw.

"Now seriously, stay here while I go get help," Jack said. "I promise I'll come back."

Loco raised his claw higher and shouted, "Dog!"

Jack put out his index finger, and Loco hopped on. The parrot settled himself on Jack's shoulder. Great. He had only been stranded for one night, and he already looked like some kind of pirate.

Trees grew low and thick on the southern slope leading inland. Jack ducked under some branches and climbed over others. He detoured around dense clusters of bamboo. Jack reached into his jeans pocket and rubbed his Saint Anthony medal. The saint would find somebody.

After a quarter of an hour trekking uphill, the ground leveled out. Jack headed north, looking for a break in the trees that might show the rooftops of a town or a village.

The trees thinned out as he came to a steep incline littered with rocks. Jack scrambled to the top and turned around. The island dropped away below him. Green trees, white sand, gray rocks, and blue sea.

No rooftops.

The island was uninhabited.

CHAPTER 7

In which Jack becomes a homesteader

Jack cupped his hands around his eyes. Steep cliffs ran along the eastern side of the island, dropping into the sea. On the western side, where Jack had come ashore, a long, spotted lump floated outside the reef. Its heavy body dipped below the surface and came back up again. The whale shark.

Jack sank down on a flat rock. He was on a deserted island with a parrot. A whale shark cruised along the shore, waiting for him to put one toe in the water. His worst imaginings of what could go wrong while traveling with his parents had come true.

But somebody would come and get him. His parents had said "directly." That was British for "right away." Jack only hoped they would hire professionals instead of coming up with their own plan. Professionals could chart the course of the lost boat using mathematical formulas. They might even fly over the island with helicopters.

Jack stood up. He just had to survive long enough to get rescued. The most important thing was to find water. He had seen a show where a family adrift in the Pacific had been forced to drink their own urine to survive. That same night he had woken up shouting, "It does *not* taste okay!"

Jack walked parallel to the eastern cliffs, pausing every few feet. Then, over the breeze rustling through the bamboo, he heard something. A faint splashing sound.

Loco dug his claws in as Jack ducked into the brush. The splashing grew louder. Jack paused to listen again, then pushed aside a long, leafy branch.

A dark hole appeared in the side of the earth below him. Water dribbled over the edges of a large, flat rock. Jack scrambled down to the rock shelf and filled his soda bottle. When he had half a bottle, he drank it down.

He refilled his bottle and gulped until his stomach stuck out.

Loco stomped around in the shallow pool and threw water on his feathers. He shook them out, spraying water in Jack's face.

"Thank you," Jack said. "That was very considerate."

Loco bobbed on his shoulder as Jack trudged back to the other side of the island. Jack wished he were more athletic. Aunt Julia used to tell him to go outside and exercise, but he had spent a lot of his free time reading or playing video games with Zack. Had he known his parents would abandon him at sea, he would have devised a year-round fitness program.

Jack was panting by the time he began the descent back to the beach. Loco hopped up and down on his shoulder. "Bad dog! Bad dog!"

"Why are you complaining?" Jack asked.

"You haven't done anything but ride along."

Loco scrambled down his arm and marched toward a tree. The parrot poked at something on the ground.

Jack said, "What is that?"

The bird's beak tore through the skin of a large purple fruit. It wasn't anything Jack had seen before, but it smelled like mango.

Jack reached down to pick it up. The parrot nipped his hand.

"Ow," Jack cried.

He looked up into the tree. Heavy fruit hung above him, like purple moons orbiting a leafy sky.

Jack grabbed one and peeled the skin back. It wasn't like any mango he'd had before. The ones his aunt used to buy were yellow and stringy. But this fruit had that same perfumey taste.

"Hah," Jack said, juice dribbling down his chin. "We have water and food. Finally, my luck is changing. Good eye, Loco."

Jack pulled three more pieces of fruit from the tree. He cupped the mangoes and his water bottle in his T-shirt and picked his way down the slope to the beach. Loco followed him, chanting "Bad dog!"

● ● ●

Jack washed his shirt out in the surf and hung it on a tree branch to dry. He might be shipwrecked, but that didn't mean he had to turn into a slob. He had water and food, and he had done the laundry. What next?

Somewhere to sleep. Somewhere away from rough weather and coconuts. Somewhere not so close to the water, where a certain sneaky whale shark might snatch him right off the sand. Jack had seen killer whales do that to seals on Animal Planet. One moment, a seal frolicked in the waves. The next, it was gone.

Jack scrambled up the rubbly slope to the hole partially shielded by the tree. He pushed aside the branches and saw a cavern the size of a single-car garage. A shaft of light from a hole in the roof lit up the back.

Jack ducked through the opening and stood up. It felt cool and dry inside.

"Perfect," he said.

He snapped off the overhanging branches that screened the entrance until he could walk in and out without ducking.

* * *

Four trips later, Jack had hauled everything from the boat into the cave. He arranged his supplies and stood back to survey his effort.

On one side of the cave, Jack had spread the tarp out on the ground, laid the towels on top, and set a life jacket down as a pillow. He had made a nest for Loco by scrunching up another life jacket and tying it into a circle.

On the other side, Jack had placed two stones a few feet apart and rested a piece of driftwood on top. He tore off the plastic cover of *Snorkel Now! Caribbean Edition*. The book came with a waterproof slate and a pencil. He set the book and the dive slate on the shelf. Then he lined up his packs of M&M's, bags of potato chips, and bottles of soda, and put the box of Spider-Man Band-Aids and tubes of Neosporin next to them. Across from the library-kitchen-medical area, he stacked the snorkel fins, masks, the mesh bag, and the rope.

It would be good enough until someone came. Jack could watch the sea right from the entrance of his cave. That seemed strange. *His cave.* It wasn't *his* cave. He wouldn't be stranded long enough for that.

Loco marched in and perched himself on the driftwood shelf. The parrot didn't seem that impressed.

"Really?" Jack said. "And you could do better? I even made you a bed. A thank-you would be nice."

Jack picked up the dive slate and wrote:

Name of castaway: Jack Berenson
Things trying to kill Jack:
parents (as usual)
coconuts
whale shark

He lay down on the tarp, put his hands behind his head, and stared at the ceiling of the cave. His muscles ached. Jack supposed he hadn't exercised so much in his whole life. His

face felt hot from so much time in the sun.

If Diana could see him now, what would she think? She would probably be impressed. When Jack told her the story of what happened, it wouldn't be necessary to mention anything he hadn't done exactly right. Like forgetting to put gas on the checklist.

He might become a celebrity. Who else at Henderson Middle School had ever been shipwrecked? If he got interviewed for the news, Jack could show the reporters how he got water and food and set up a shelter. He would be humble and say, "I'm not a hero. I just did what anybody would do."

Jack sat up and took *Snorkel Now! Caribbean Edition* to the entrance of the cave. Popping M&M's in his mouth, he flipped through the pages. The introduction was about snorkel equipment and how it worked. The rest was about sea creatures.

Coral: Looks like a plant but is actually an animal. Touching coral could kill it. Meanwhile, people who accidentally touched fire coral would feel as if their skin had burst into flames.

Stingrays: People should shuffle their feet on the sand so the ray doesn't get surprised and sting them.

Barracuda: People should not wear shiny jewelry that the barracuda might think is a small fish. That way, the barracuda won't bite off the body part the jewelry is attached to.

There were a lot of misunderstandings in the ocean.

Whale shark: *The whale shark is known as the gentle giant of the sea. It can grow to lengths of forty feet and reach nearly fifteen tons. It is a filter feeder, primarily subsisting on plankton. It is friendly to divers and snorkelers. The country of Belize knows it as "Sapodilla Tom" because of its regular appearances near the Sapodilla Cayes.*

Jack dropped the book.

"Um, Loco," he said, walking into the cave and picking up the dive slate, "we made a slight mistake about whale sharks. It turns out we are not actually being stalked."

Loco said, "Whatever."

Jack crossed *whale shark* off his list of things trying to kill him. "I think that whale shark pushed us to land," Jack said. "We could have floated right by this island. He didn't accidentally push us into the channel—he did it on purpose. He was trying to help us. I think."

* * *

The next day, Jack attempted to open coconuts while keeping one eye out for boats and helicopters. He chipped at the coconuts with the sharp end of a bamboo pole. He banged them on rocks. He soaked them in seawater to see if they would soften up. They were indestructible.

The whale shark cruised along Jack's side of the island, its mouth opening wide to scoop in plankton. Jack decided to call him Tom, like people from Belize did. He figured the whale shark was already used to that name.

Jack took the cooler up to the waterfall and hauled it back half full of water. Loco had gotten sick of all the running around the island and stayed in the cave where it was cool.

Hauling himself up the ridge for the last rescue boat check of the day, Jack realized the climb had gotten harder each time. He knew it was because he hadn't had proper food. Mangoes, potato chips, and chocolate were not exactly a balanced diet. His home economics teacher would be disgusted. At least he had fruit so he wouldn't get scurvy.

Tom glided by the channel, looking like he didn't have a care in the world. Which, Jack supposed, he didn't.

"Hi, Tom," Jack shouted. "Sorry for the mix-up earlier. It's just that you look . . . and you know, with a name like whale shark . . . it was easy to think . . . Well, anyway, sorry about that."

Tom's tail fin slapped the surface.

A low hum rumbled in the distance. Jack jerked around to see a boat cruising along the coastline, toward his beach.

CHAPTER 8

In which Jack discovers why his parents would not be suited for a career in the Coast Guard

Jack's dad was at the helm of a white outboard speedboat. His mom stood behind him, her blonde hair blowing in the wind.

"Hey," Jack cried. "Hey, I'm up here!"

The boat slowed as it neared the channel.

"Yes! It's me! Look! I'm standing right here!"

His mom pointed at Tom.

The boat swung around and settled into a drift near the whale shark.

"No! Do not get distracted!" Jack shouted. "I'm right here! I'm standing at the top of the ridge. Turn around!"

His mom reached over the side of the boat and ran her hand along Tom's back. One distraction and Jack's parents totally forgot what they were supposed to be doing.

Jack raced through the trees down to the shoreline. He flung himself over low branches and dove under the higher ones. The beach was straight ahead.

His parents had turned away from Tom. His dad picked up binoculars and scanned the island.

Jack waved wildly through the trees.

His dad lowered the binoculars and shrugged. His mom shook her head. The boat turned and sped out to sea.

Jack burst onto the beach. He shouted after the boat, waved his arms, and threw coconuts into the water. They didn't turn around.

He kicked the trunk of a palm tree.

Loco's distant voice piped up from the cave. "Whatever."

His parents hadn't hired professionals. They were racing around on their own. Who had come up with that idea? Probably both of them.

Their worst ideas were usually a team effort.

Jack climbed up to the cave and sat at the entrance. Now that his parents believed they had searched the area, how long would it take them to come back again?

"Loco, I'm afraid we'll be here longer than we thought. I might have to become an outdoors person."

● ● ●

That afternoon, the sun rose high in a cloudless sky. The sand burned; Jack could feel the heat through his sneakers. If he ever got off the island, he would move to Alaska and lie in the snow all day. He would lie in the snow naked.

Jack downed a bottle of water and poured some into a shell for Loco. Even in the cave, his skin felt hot. Jack had avoided going into the bay. He didn't like the idea of live fish swimming underneath him. Now that he might be living on the island long-term, he decided he better get used to it.

Jack grabbed a mask and a set of fins. He wanted to be able to see what was underneath him, and the fins would help him execute an emergency evacuation.

At the water's edge, Jack put his mask around his neck and waded in. The water tickled his hot skin. He stopped when it reached his waist.

With his mask and snorkel in place, Jack bent over and put his face in the water. His breath sounded loud through the snorkel. He pushed off the sand and floated facedown.

The sand and the sea grass were as clear to him as if they'd been up on the beach. Tiny creatures, tucked in round brown shells, lurked in the grass. Jack supposed they hid in the vegetation so they wouldn't get eaten. That's what he would do if he were that small and had to live in the ocean.

He cautiously kicked toward the reef. If he saw a stingray or a shark, he'd turn back.

Jack swam to the north side of the channel. A patch of sand, fifteen feet deep, was enclosed on three sides by walls of coral. Greenish globes looking like oversized brains squatted on the sand. Hollow tubes in poppy red and lilac jutted out from the reef wall. A school of navy-colored

fish with flat, oval bodies glided past Jack's mask.

He ducked beneath the water and kicked down until pressure built in his ears. Jack had read about that. He pinched his nose and blew like the book had said to. A slight pop came out of his right ear and then the left.

Jack practiced kicking and clearing his ears until he could swim down to the bottom. Red-and-white-striped shrimp burrowed into the sand, snapping oversized claws at Jack's mask. Tiny blue-and-yellow fish darted in and out of the coral. An octopus tucked itself into a crevice, its eight legs curled underneath its oversize oblong head.

The reef was an underwater metropolis.

* * *

"Loco, you won't believe this," Jack said, stepping through the entrance of the cave. "It turns out I'm a natural at snorkeling."

"Whatever," Loco said.

"I know! Who would have thought? I was worried that I might get eaten or be drowned. I think Aunt Julia would have worried about that too. I wish I could tell her we were wrong."

Jack eyed the kitchen area. "We should celebrate. It's not every day that I find out I'm good at a sport."

He popped a soda bottle open. "The last one and we're going to drink it. We'll have potato chips too."

"Bad dog," Loco muttered.

"You're right. It's not the safest choice. Not while we're relying on my parents to rescue us. But I'm doing it anyway."

Jack ripped open a bag of chips. Loco waddled over to him and looked up.

He laid a chip on the tarp. Loco pecked at it and shouted, "Dog!"

Jack stuffed potato chips in his mouth. "You're right. It's really good."

* * *

Jack lost track of how long he'd been on the island. The daylight hours passed quickly as he followed his daily routine. At dawn, he would climb the ridge to scout for boats and to yell Tom a good-morning. Sometimes the whale shark was close to the reef; sometimes he was farther out to sea.

When Jack would leave the ridge, he'd pass by the waterfall and fill up the cooler. Then he would stop by the mango tree and pick a few fruit. Back in the cave, he'd shake the sand off his bed, lie down with a mango, and read *Snorkel Now! Caribbean Edition.*

In the afternoon, when the heat was at its worst, Jack would snorkel in the bay.

Jack used the mesh equipment bag as a net to catch fish and dried the strips of meat in the blazing sun. His catches were small, and the fish jerky was chewy and disgusting, but at least it was protein.

Loco's clipped wings had begun to grow in, and the bird would spend a lot of time flapping around the beach, making valiant takeoffs and flopping into the sand. The parrot had learned to say his name. After each crash landing, he would right himself, shake out his feathers, and cry, "Loco!"

Jack had fashioned a roof over the entrance of the cave by resting palm leaves across the branches up above. At sunset, he would sit on the rock ledge, gnawing on dried fish and waiting for the stars to come out.

* * *

As the days wore on, Jack became obsessed with food that didn't taste like fish or mangoes. He invented a game called What's on the Menu? He'd squeeze his eyes shut and picture himself seated at a restaurant. The waiter would hand him a large white menu with nothing written on it. Then Jack would use his mind to write what he wanted.

DOUBLE CHEESEBURGER W/ FRIES
A GALLON OF ROCKY ROAD ICE CREAM
TURKEY CLUB SANDWICH WITH EXTRA MAYONNAISE
A BOTTLE OF VERY COLD YOO-HOO

The last bag of potato chips continued to sit on the cave shelf. As long as Jack refused to open it, he had not yet officially run out of rations.

One night, Jack ended What's on the Menu? by saying good-bye to a large pepperoni pizza that had been floating around in his mind. The cove below him shimmered in the moonlight like rippling blue satin. Jack realized that if he rigged a swing, he could jump in whenever he wanted to, without having to scramble down the rocks.

Jack grabbed the rope from the cave, looped it around a sturdy branch hanging over the water, and tied it with four knots. He pulled to make sure it would hold.

The fifteen-foot drop seemed higher to Jack now that he was preparing to jump off. He could imagine Aunt Julia worrying about broken legs and cracked-open heads.

Loco marched out of the cave, looked at the rope, and said, "Whatever."

"Oh, really?" Jack said. He grabbed the rope and yelled, "Watch this!"

He leapt off the rocks. The bay spun underneath him as he arced through the air. Then the rope started its swing in the opposite direction.

If he didn't let go, he would crash into the rocks.

He loosened his grip.

* * *

Jack tumbled through the air and plummeted into the water. He kicked to the surface.

Loco peered down from the ledge.

"You see?" Jack cried. "I did it."

He scrambled back up the rocks. Now he would try jumping off with the snorkel gear. Jack put his mask around his neck and held his fins close to his body. He grabbed the rope, ran off the ledge, and plunged into the sea. No broken leg or cracked-open head.

* * *

The next morning, Jack climbed the ridge in the pink of dawn. Beneath him, Tom rolled in circles. He looked like he was having a good time.

Wait a minute. What was Tom doing?

The whale shark thrashed close to the reef.

"Don't do that, Tom," Jack shouted. "That coral will cut you up!"

He wondered about Tom. The whale shark lived in the ocean. Didn't he know coral was sharp?

Why wasn't Tom cruising along, scooping up plankton, like he usually did? The shark's dorsal fin broke the surface of the water. Jack spotted something clinging to it. Something brown and ropey.

A net.

CHAPTER 9

In which Jack discovers that whale sharks can be unpredictable

"Loco," Jack cried, climbing to the cave. "Tom needs help."

"Dog?" Loco screeched.

"I said, 'Tom needs help!'"

Tom rose in the water and crashed down on the surface again.

"Just calm down and try to untangle yourself," Jack called out. "Loco, I have to go out and see if I can do anything."

He grabbed his mask and fins. "Tom will kill himself on the coral if he keeps this up. He got us to the island. We have to help him if we can."

Jack swung out on the rope and dropped into the sea. He yanked his fins on and kicked across the bay.

The channel loomed in front of him, funneling four-foot swells. Jack put his snorkel in and kicked. A wave picked him up and threw him back. He kicked harder, inching forward as the sea pushed him dangerously close to the coral wall.

He got through to the open sea, and a wave broke over Jack's head. His snorkel filled with

water. Jack ripped it out of his mouth. Another wave broke and pushed him under. He was drowning.

Jack's fins brushed something solid, and he was heaved out of the sea. Smooth, spotted flesh stretched out underneath him.

Tom.

Jack lay on Tom's back, coughing out seawater. He caught his breath and pulled his mask down around his neck. The net sticking to Tom had looped around the shark's dorsal fin.

Jack patted Tom's back. "Now, Tom, I'm just going to get that net off your fin. Do not thrash us onto the reef or anything, okay?"

He inched back toward Tom's dorsal fin.

"Good, Tom," Jack said. "Just hold steady. Exactly like you're doing."

The cause of Tom's problem looked like an old and rotting fishing net with bits of trash tangled in it. Jack grabbed the edge of the net and tugged. Stuck.

"Okay, Tom, I need to get a little closer."

Jack crouched on the whale's back as they rode up and down the swells.

There. There was the reason Tom couldn't get loose. A hole in the net had snagged the tip of Tom's fin. Jack tugged the net upward until it came loose, then pulled it all the way off. The net slipped into the sea and floated away with the current.

"We did it, Tom," he cried. "It's off! Now stay away from that net so you don't get caught in it again." Jack lay on the shark's back, looking toward its massive head. Tom's smooth flesh felt cold on his skin. He patted the shark and said,

"Good job, Tom."

Tom arched his back. Jack slid toward Tom's head.

"Hey! Cut that out!"

Tom's head disappeared underwater. The shark was diving. Jack jumped off and kicked away. Tom's dorsal fin submerged; his tail fin followed. He was gone.

Jack twisted around. He was farther from land than he had realized, and the current was pulling him past the channel. He put on his mask and snorkel and began to kick. The sea beneath him looked bottomless. Tom had become a dark shadow, swimming deeper and deeper.

Jack fought against the current, using the long, powerful kicks he had practiced inside the reef. It felt as if he were hardly getting anywhere. If he stopped kicking for a moment, the powerful sea swept him backward.

Kick by kick, he finally neared the channel. A wave pushed him forward, then pulled him back again. Another wave tossed him surging into the bay.

Jack crawled up on the beach, breathing

hard, the warmth of the sand sinking into his body.

* * *

Back in the cave, Jack lay on the tarp, exhausted. "I know what you're thinking, Loco. I shouldn't have done it."

"Whatever."

"In the end, though, it worked out. There were times I was worried. I won't lie about that. And I don't know why Tom dived down and left me by myself. That didn't seem very grateful." Jack paused. "I suppose I'll never really know what Tom was thinking. All I can do is add what he did to the rules of engagement for whale sharks. Rule: no matter what else is going on, a whale shark might suddenly decide to dive."

"Whatever."

Jack twisted around and looked at Loco. "You know, you should really stop being so cynical."

* * *

The next morning, Jack ran to the top of the ridge and scanned the sea.

Tom looked good as new. He drifted along the reef, his mouth wide open, eating his plankton breakfast.

A white outboard sped around the far tip of the island.

"Hey," he cried. "Look up! You have to look up! I'm right here! Again!"

The boat slowed to a drift outside of the channel.

Jack's dad scanned the beach with binoculars. His mom stood at the back of the boat, shooting off signal flares. Bursts of orangey-red light spattered the sky like bucketfuls of paint.

"What are you doing?" Jack shouted. "Look up!"

Jack grabbed a heavy rock and tried to throw it into the sea. It rolled down into the trees.

His mom grabbed his dad's arm. She pointed to the sky, then sent up another flare. They watched it explode and fizzle out, then high-fived each other.

"Don't get distracted!" Jack said. "Look up! Up!"

Arms pumping, Jack sprinted down the slope

to the beach, weaving around stands of bamboo.

He burst out from the trees and jumped up and down on the sand. "Now, seriously!" he yelled. "You can't miss me this time!"

Jack's dad looked toward the island. His dad grabbed his mom's arm and pointed to Jack.

"Hold on, Son. Help is on the way!" he shouted. The boat headed toward land at full throttle.

"The channel!" Jack yelled. "It's over there. To the left! To the left!"

"Yes, we see you, Jack," his dad shouted. "We're not idiots!"

The boat rode up onto the reef with a splintering sound. Jack's parents were thrown to the deck. They staggered up, and his mom brushed the hair off her face.

Water flooded the stern. The spot where the engine had been was now a gaping hole.

"Bit of a technical problem," his dad called.

Jack stood motionless. His parents had wrecked the boat.

CHAPTER 10

In which Jack hauls in two new castaways

"No worries, luv," Jack's mom shouted. "We'll get this sorted out directly."

"Don't move," Jack yelled. "Don't make any decisions or come up with any plans!"

Loco marched down to the beach. Jack raced past him and muttered, "Don't even pretend you're shocked," then sprinted up to the cave and grabbed his snorkel gear.

Jack gripped the rope and swung into the water. He had to get to the channel before the boat sank. Jack did not want to even imagine what kind of plan his parents might come up with if that happened. They might decide to try to swim back to Lee Beach.

His dad's muffled voice drifted over the water. "Did he just jump off a cliff?"

Jack paused in front of the channel. The waves were higher than they had been the last time. He looked underwater.

The passage through the reef to open ocean dropped down thirty feet, surrounded by dead, colorless coral. A few scraggly plants clung to the channel walls, swaying back and forth with the surge.

A dark shadow appeared. As it moved closer, Jack realized it was Tom.

The whale shark's tail fin waved gently in the center of the channel.

Jack did not know the rules of engagement for grabbing a whale shark's tail fin, but he supposed he was about to find out. He took a deep breath and kicked.

Jack grabbed the end of Tom's fin. The whale shark moved slowly forward. Jack held on, coasting up and down on the waves.

The shark pulled Jack through the passage.

Blue, bottomless water appeared beneath him. He was through to open ocean. Jack let go of Tom's fin.

The shark's tail fin gave a powerful swish, and Tom disappeared into the depths.

Jack kicked over to his parent's boat.

"Look at you, rascal," his mom said, hauling Jack onto the wrecked boat. "Jumping off cliffs and swimming around with whale sharks . . ."

"We've got to get off before the boat sinks," Jack said, panting. He pointed to the life jackets tucked under the seat. "Put those on. It's rough in the channel."

"That's one idea," his dad said. "But wouldn't you rather take the raft?"

"What raft?" Jack asked.

His mom pointed to a heap of rubber at the bow. "That one, luv. It's an inflatable. We just work the foot pump and off we go."

"Why didn't you tell me that before I swam out here?" Jack sputtered.

"You didn't give us a moment, Son," his dad said. "You just jumped right into the water. Bit of a shock, really."

"How did you even think to bring a raft?" Jack said. "I mean, that's not . . . like something you would do."

"Ah," his dad said, rubbing his hands together. "In between searches for you, we did an awful lot of thinking about checklists. You know, since that first one went amiss. We decided a raft should be on the list. And also, a hairbrush for your mom. The wind does terrible things to her hair."

"Oh, but, Richard," his mom said, glancing at his dad, "one item on the list won't do us any good."

"What?" Jack asked.

Jack's dad pointed to a red plastic container tucked beneath the console. "The spare petrol. And we thought we'd been so clever. Just put the petrol on the skiff, and off we go. Now this boat is wrecked, and you've lost the skiff. We've gone from two boats to no boats. We didn't see that coming."

His mom glanced at the rubber raft and said, "It's going to be a long paddle home."

"I didn't lose the skiff," Jack said. "It's in

the lagoon."

"Well, really, Jack," his dad said, "it's a miracle we found you at all. We've been racing around looking for the skiff. Naturally we thought, you find the skiff, you find the boy."

"Why would you hide it?" his mom asked.

"It doesn't matter," Jack said. "Don't you see? I have a boat, and you have gas. That's how we get home."

"He's on to something, Claire," his dad said.

* * *

They inflated the raft, loaded the spare gas container, and paddled hard through the waves in the channel. On the beach, Loco marched over to Jack's dad, shouted, "Bad dog!" and bit his sneaker.

"Ow," his dad cried. "Oh, hello, you! Jack, you saved the bird. Well done." He turned and said, "Claire, here's something odd. My stomach ailment is cured."

"Mine too!" his mom said.

"What was wrong with your stomachs?" Jack asked, searching the sea for Tom.

"Your dad and I caught a terrible stomach virus," his mom said.

"Absolutely wretched," his dad said, "it came on directly after the . . . drift snorkeling mishap. Almost as if we'd breathed it in. A terrible, twisting knot. Enough to drive you mad."

"And now it's gone," his mom said. "Gosh, Jack, I hope we weren't contagious. I wouldn't like you to get it."

"It wasn't a virus," Jack said. "You were worried. That's why your stomach hurt. It happens to me all the time."

"Does it?" his mom asked.

"That's awful," his dad said.

"Yes," Jack answered, "it has been."

"Richard, I think Jack's right," his mom said. "Remember what we said right before the pain struck? If it had been us drifting away, it would've been a bit of a laugh. But somehow, because it was Jack, it wasn't."

"True. And every time we talked about what might have happened to him, the ache got worse," his dad said.

"It did!"

"Well," his dad said, "it's a happy day that our worries are over. Let's get the petrol on the skiff, and off we go."

"We can't leave now," Jack said. "It'll be dark in an hour!"

"Richard," his mom said, "this sounds like something that should be on the checklist. Time of day."

"Very sensible," his dad said. "Right then, let's huddle under a tree and wait for daybreak."

Jack shook his head. "Sitting under a palm tree is like playing Russian roulette with coconuts. C'mon, follow me." He picked up Loco and headed back to the cave. His parents scrambled up the rocks behind him.

"Look at this," his mom said. "Just as cozy as can be." She pointed to the shelf. "It even has a makeshift kitchen."

"Are those crisps?" his dad asked.

"Don't touch the potato chips," Jack said. "We'll divide them up for dinner."

His mom picked up the dive slate "Ooh, Jack, you've been writing..." She trailed off, then whispered, "Richard, come look at this."

"At once, luv," his dad said, giving the potato chips a wistful glance. "Ah, very resourceful, Jack. Writing to keep busy. What? 'Things trying to kill Jack'? 'Parents . . . as usual.'"

They turned to Jack.

Jack had forgotten about the list of things trying to kill him. He was about to tell them it was just a joke. But it wasn't a joke.

"I'm sorry if that hurts your feelings," Jack said. "I probably should have written 'accidentally' instead of 'as usual.' I know you don't do dangerous things on purpose, but you still do them."

"Jack," his mom said, "you don't really think we meant for this to happen?"

"No, but it happened anyway. You weren't careful, and I had to live with the consequences."

"Bad dog," Loco said.

"Richard," his mom said, "has the master plan failed?"

"Impossible," his dad answered. "It's the master plan. The plan to end all plans."

"But look at him. Jack should be happy by now, and he doesn't seem like he is."

His dad furrowed his brow. "Should we tweak the master plan?"

"What master plan?" Jack asked.

CHAPTER 11

In which Jack becomes acquainted with the master plan

"*The* master plan," his dad said.

"I don't know what you're talking about," Jack said.

"Of course you do, luv," his mom said. "Everybody knows about the master plan."

"No, they don't," Jack answered.

"Certainly Aunt Julia talked about the master plan?" his dad asked.

His mom glanced at his dad. "Julia didn't actually approve of the master plan."

"But we talked about it every time we saw you," his dad said.

Jack thought about that. His parents had always talked about this plan or that plan. But one plan pretty much mixed with another in Jack's head. They were all just the "we're leaving again" plans.

"Okay, what's the master plan?"

"Well," Jack's mom said, "by the time you were born, we had already been through a few different careers."

"Careers?" Jack said. "What careers?"

"Let's see," his mom said. "We were forest fire lookouts for a while."

"Until the fire," his dad said, shaking his head.

"We house-sat for a soap opera star once."

"He got a little melodramatic over one tiny gas leak, but that's Hollywood for you."

"We tried crop dusting."

"Finding the landing strip is harder than you'd think."

"When you were very little, we were chimney sweeps."

"Who would have thought it would take two fire companies to get me out of that last chimney?" his dad said.

Jack suddenly understood why he had soot on his face in so many of his baby pictures. He had always wondered about that.

"So, it was all a bit of a laugh. We were just going along, certain we would hit upon the perfect jobs for us," his mom said.

"But you turned three, and we still couldn't afford to buy you a pony."

"We realized we had better buckle down and get serious."

"Actually, Julia said we had better buckle down and get serious."

"We analyzed everything that had gone wrong in our different careers and came to two remarkable conclusions."

"One," his dad said, "if we kept going on the way we had been, we'd spend our entire lives in and out of court. American judges have no sense of humor."

"And two, we were clearly not suited to have bosses," his mom said. "Especially not American bosses. They are so particular!"

"Those conclusions *are* pretty remarkable," Jack said.

"Yes, we saw that at the time," his dad said. "You, meanwhile, were getting old enough to notice that you did not have a pony."

"All the facts pointed in one direction," his mom said. "If we wanted to live the American dream, we needed to look outside America."

"Once we figured that out, the rest was easy."

Jack's dad reached into his pocket and pulled out a plastic pouch. "Waterproof. Keeps the plan nice and dry." He opened the pouch, pulled out a dirty and crumpled sheet of paper, and smoothed the creases.

Jack took the paper and read it.

Our son Jack, named after the courageous Jack of beanstalk fame, just turned three years old. We are determined to buckle down and get serious so he can have a really fun life. We both grew up wishing for things we didn't get (ponies!) and getting things we didn't want (shots!) and have figured out how our parents went wrong. They didn't have a master plan. Here's ours: Jack will have a pony, he will have as much candy as he

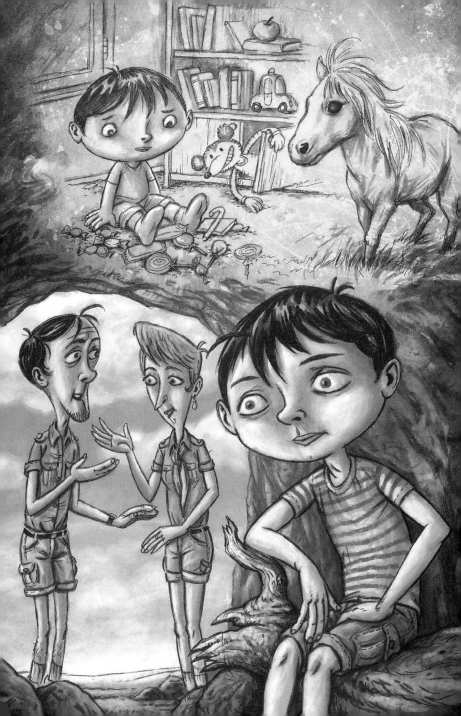

wants, bring as many animals home as he wants, go to school only when he feels like it, sleep out in the yard in the summer, take long canoe trips by himself, ski the Alps, and have his own Easy-Bake Oven in his room so he can make cookies in the middle of the night. He will not have a bedtime or any homework. He will have the childhood we wish we'd had.

"Of course, you already had some of those things. No bedtime and lots of candy," his dad said.

"But we had to get more money," his mom added.

"So we left you with Aunt Julia and off we went to make our fortune," his dad said. "Though, when we look back now, it's taking longer than expected."

"Ages longer," his mom said. "We figured you'd be with Julia for six months, tops."

"And here it's been nearly eight years . . ."

"But every time we got discouraged," his mom said, "we'd think: remember, we're doing this for Jack."

Jack said, "I've never wanted a pony."

"Every kid wants a pony," his mom said.

"No, they don't."

"How about a llama?"

"No."

"Well, whatever it is you do want," his dad said, "we'll buy it for you directly."

What did Jack want from his parents? He wasn't sure. But he knew where to start. He said, "I want you to stop doing crazy things."

"Stop doing crazy things," his mom said. "We can do that, Richard. Assuming he spells out exactly what he means by crazy?"

"I'm sure we can, luv. We're the Berensons. We can do anything."

"Done. No more crazy things," his mom said.

Jack got up and paced around the cave.

"What is it, Jack?"

"Son?"

So his parents had promised not to do anything crazy anymore. Just like that. Now everything was fine?

"I'm sorry," Jack said, "but this is ridiculous.

I want to have homework, and I want to get enough sleep. I have never thought about taking a long canoe trip by myself. Okay, maybe the Easy-Bake Oven is a good idea. But who would leave their kid with a relative, run around the world trying to get rich, and call it a master plan? And you named me after 'Jack and the Beanstalk'? Who does that?"

"Us?" his mom said. Jack's mom swiped at her eyes. His dad stared at the ground. They didn't look how they usually looked—all cheery, no worries. They looked more like . . . real people. Like Aunt Julia.

"Could've been worse," his dad mumbled. "It's not as though we named him after Jack the Ripper."

His mom said, "Jack. All of our plans have been for you."

"They're not for me," Jack said. "If they were for me, you wouldn't have been gone all the time. You would have noticed when I was missing for an entire day. You wouldn't have left me on a boat with no gas."

His mom looked like she wanted to speak.

Jack waved his hands to stop her. "It's okay, I'll get over it. I just thought, you know, that I should say it at least once."

The cave was silent.

"Jack," his dad said, "we may have gone about this all backwards and sideways, but how could we have known you wouldn't love the master plan?"

"We thought it was great," his mom said.

His parents really believed the master plan had been a good idea.

"Well, even if that's true, I don't know what we could do now," Jack said. "You're just not safe to be around. I can't even imagine what dangerous thing you'll come up with next. You never think ahead and try to figure out what might happen."

His dad cleared his throat. "Now, Son, point taken. But since the drift snorkeling incident, your mom and I have made great strides. We brought petrol, a hairbrush, and a rubber raft with us on this go."

"We even packed a lunch. Although we left that on the dock," his mom said.

"And," his dad continued, "we don't want to go overboard on the whole thinking-ahead idea. We don't want to think ahead so much we never actually do anything. I'll admit, our master plan has not been the success we had assumed it would be. But we don't want to spend our whole lives fretting about . . . disasters."

His mom nodded. "Like imagining Lee Beach is surrounded by bull sharks."

"You see, Jack," his dad said, "when your mom and I noticed those dark patches in the water, we didn't leap to that conclusion."

Jack's face burned. "They could have been sharks."

"They also could have been treasure chests," his mom said.

"Of course, when we swam out there, we realized we were mistaken," his dad said. "We should have known that no pirate is going to leave his treasure in plain view. He's going to bury it."

Jack stared at his mom and dad. How could he and his parents have both looked at sea grass and come up with such different ideas? Jack understood how he had arrived at sharks. The first thing a sane beachgoer was going to worry about was man-eaters. But treasure chests? He would never understand what went on in his parents' heads.

Then Jack remembered Tom. Tom had left him stranded in the ocean, and Jack hadn't understood why. Jack had realized he would never know what Tom was thinking. All he could do was figure out his rules of engagement for whale sharks.

That was it. He needed rules of engagement for Richard and Claire Berenson. "We have to agree on family rules," Jack said. "So we all know what's okay and not okay. Then there won't be so many surprises."

"Rules?" his dad said. "What do you know, Claire? Rules are the last thing we would have put in the master plan. How could we have guessed the boy would want rules?"

"He's turning out to be very unpredictable," his mom said.

Jack opened the bag of potato chips and divided up the meal. Loco finished his first and then glared at everybody. Jack lay on the tarp, licking the salt off a chip, with his mom on one side and his dad on the other.

"First rule," Jack said. "Whenever you go to do something, take a moment and think: Is there any danger? What could happen? After you've thought about it, you can decide whether or not to do it."

"Agreed," his mom said. "Think before doing."

His dad said, "Rule number two: When thinking before doing, don't get sidetracked predicting disaster. The Berensons have nerves of steel." He paused. "Son, you can start with nerves of aluminum and work your way up."

"Agreed," Jack said, "no more expecting disaster. But I'll still keep an eye out for bull sharks. Anybody that isn't worried about them is just not dealing with reality. Rule three: All adults in the family must have jobs. Get-rich-quick schemes are a hobby, not a career."

"That's harsh," his dad said.

"Jack," his mom said, "now is probably not a good time to start on that rule. We're certain pirate treasure is buried back on the island."

"This is what I'm talking about," Jack said, sternly. "Left on your own, you'd spend the next six months digging holes, come up with nothing, and then say it seemed like such a sure thing."

"When you put it like that, it doesn't sound so . . ." his mom trailed off.

"I smell a compromise," his dad said. "We run the snorkel business five days a week and dig for treasure two days a week. How about that, Jack?"

"If that's how you want to spend your weekend, that's fine with me. Rule four: I spend my summer vacations in Pennsylvania with Zack. I feel a growth spurt coming on, and I'll need to be there after it happens."

His dad rolled over on his side. "Is this about a girl?" he asked.

"Don't get distracted, Dad," Jack said. "Focus on the rules."

It took two more hours to work out the rest of the rules. Jack and his parents spent the majority of time haggling over exactly how long a typical workday was supposed to be. Jack's parents felt that three hours should be sufficient. Jack thought they should work ten hours to make up for all the years they hadn't worked at all. They finally settled on five hours.

Jack also got them to agree to rent Ms. Seldie's apartment. He felt Seldie would be a good influence on his parents. And on himself.

His mom stretched out on the tarp. "Good, it's all sorted," she said.

As Jack lay there, a lingering idea kept bothering him. The rules didn't cover every possible thing that could happen. His family needed a way to make decisions.

• • •

The next morning, Jack's dad pulled the boat out of the lagoon and his mom carried the supplies down from the cave. Jack sat at the entrance and called down to the beach. "Don't start the engine until I'm down there."

"Right," his dad called up. "I just said to your mom, the last thing we want to do is drive off before we've got Jack on the boat. We're way ahead of you there."

Jack picked up the dive slate and wrote out the Berenson family decision-making rules.

If you are Jack, don't assume the worst will happen. Imagine what Richard and Claire would do and then take out the life-threatening parts.

If you are Richard and Claire, don't assume everything will be fine. Try to imagine what Jack would do. If Jack would never do what you're thinking about doing, that is a warning sign!

If we all follow the rules, we will probably survive.

Jack dug into his pocket. He walked over to the driftwood shelf and laid his Saint Anthony medal on top. The next castaway would probably need it.

CHAPTER 12

In which Jack is fortunately reunited with Seldie

Jack stood near the front of the skiff, looking for Tom. The whale shark was gone. Maybe Tom had swum off to keep somebody else company. There was no telling how many other kids were living on deserted islands for one reason or another. Or maybe Tom had just eaten up all the plankton and went somewhere else to find more. There was no way to know.

As Jack and his parents sped across the sea, he briefed them on the decision-making rules.

"Brilliant," his dad said. "Almost like a decision-making thermometer."

"It will be fascinating," his mom said. "I've always wondered what it's like to be in your head, Jack. What's your favorite food?"

Jack sighed. Getting the hang of the rules would take some practice. "Chocolate," he said over his shoulder.

"Ah," his mom said. "Mine is eggplant Parmesan. Couldn't be more different."

After an hour, the island appeared on the horizon. Jack began to pick out landmarks. There was the beach where the drift-snorkeling fiasco had begun.

Jack swung the boat into the channel and yelled, "Hold on!"

"Brilliant!" his dad shouted back.

At the dock, Jack put Loco on his shoulder and said, "Let's go find Ms. Seldie and see what she has to say."

* * *

"Miss Seldie," Jack called from the yard.

"Halloo?" Seldie called back. She leaned over the railing and laughed. "Look at you, boy. I would hardly know you. Here I was, sorry the poor boy had gone and drowned, and here you are looking like you've grown an inch. Well," she said smiling, "you did it. You lived."

"Miss Seldie," Jack said, "can we come up and talk to you? We have a plan, and we need your help."

"Now, baby, I think you need food before you go planning anything. C'mon up and eat. Then we'll see about your plans."

Seldie made them heaping plates of rice and beans. Between bites, Jack explained why he and his parents had come.

"So you see, Ms. Seldie," he said, "that way you get renters for your apartment, and my parents can get advice from you while I'm in school. You know, in case they come up with a new idea."

"Let me see if I got this straight in my mind," Miss Seldie said. "You got a set of rules to live by? I'll have to draw up my *own* rules for myself, I think. And we're going to *check* the rules. Like, there's no digging for pirate treasure on a *work*day. Though, child, I'm not sure there's a point to digging for pirate treasure on *any* day."

"I know," Jack said, "that's not me."

"That's us," his mom said. "If we find a pirate chest full of gold doubloons, we'll buy Jack a . . . well, we were going to buy him a pony, but he doesn't want one."

"Something will catch his fancy, I'm sure," his dad said.

Seldie looked hard at Jack's parents.

Jack told her, "I know what you're thinking, but it's harmless, and they're only going to do it on their days off. They've had worse plans. Trust me."

Seldie nodded. "Everybody got their little habits and inclinations, I suppose. It's not for me to tell another soul whether or not they should be digging for pirate treasure."

"If you could just make sure they don't do anything dangerous, that's what we really need," Jack said.

"Well, baby, I will say right now if I find any holes in my yard, my *cane* might get a little dangerous. At my age, I can't afford to fall into a hole and break a leg on account of anybody digging for doubloons."

"Do you hear that?" Jack said. "Mom? Dad? Absolutely no digging in the yard."

"Got it," his dad said.

"And," Seldie continued, "you got to be respectful tenants. No loud music after ten o'clock in the night."

"Done," Jack said.

"And the boy has got to go to school. A young person needs an education, you see. And he's got to do his homework, even if he'd rather be swimming in the sea or playin' a game."

"Gosh, that's hard," his mom said.

"I actually like school, Miss Seldie," Jack answered.

"Well then, child, I don't know if you got yourself a *perfect* plan. Only time will tell on that. But it seems to me that there can't be many *perfect* plans around anyhow. I'd say it's like most plans. Sometimes they work; sometimes they don't. But you never gonna know until you try the thing out."

Jack looked over at his parents. "All right, Berensons. We've got a new plan."

About the Author

Lisa Doan received a master's degree in writing for children and young adults from Vermont College of Fine Arts. As a professional vagabond, she has traveled extensively through Africa and Asia and lived on a Caribbean island for eight years. Her variety of occupations has included master scuba diving instructor, New York City headhunter, owner-chef of a Chinese restaurant, television show set medic, and deputy prothonotary of a county court. She wrote her first book during a Caribbean slow season while waiting for restaurant customers. She currently lives in Pennsylvania with a Great Dane who stares her down for biscuits.

About the Illustrator

Ivica Stevanovic has illustrated picture books such as *The Royal Treasure Measure* and *Monsters Can Mosey*, as well as book covers and graphic novels. He also teaches classes at the Academy of Art in Novi Sad, in northern Serbia. He lives in Veternik, northern Serbia, with his wife, Milica, who is also a children's illustrator, and their daughter, Katarina.

VIA AIR MAIL